Mystery *at the* Marsh

MYSTERY
at the MARSH

CAROLYN EASTWOOD

authorHOUSE®

AuthorHouse™
1663 Liberty Drive
Bloomington, IN 47403
www.authorhouse.com
Phone: 1-800-839-8640

Published by AuthorHouse 10/8/2013

ISBN: 978-1-4918-2160-2 (sc)
ISBN: 978-1-4918-2159-6 (e)

Library of Congress Control Number: 2013917315

Both cover photographs by ArcMedia, LLC

Illustrations copyrighted to author

For Corgi lovers of all ages

CHAPTER ONE

SKIPPER PEERED THROUGH THE undergrowth, his dark brown eyes fixed on two shadowy shapes. On that particular Spring morning, the fog had yet to lift, shrouding everything in a thick wet mist, but unmistakable to him were the two humans in the distance.

Reaching his side, Tango was about to step forward, when she got the "look." Skipper didn't move, but his eyes told her not only to stop, but to also stay low. Seeing that he hadn't even shaken off the sparkling dewy droplets from his nose and whiskers, Tango's eyes followed his.

Suddenly, there was the faint sound of raised voices, and through the swirling gray vapor the dogs could just make out one of the humans lunge at the other. They appeared to be wrestling, then one broke free and began to run, with the other close behind. Skipper still didn't move as the figures disappeared into the fog, but tensed and closed his eyes, almost as though he knew what was about to happen. A second later, there were two sharp cracks.

"Why are the humans letting off fireworks?" Tango whispered.

Skipper finally turned his head. "They weren't fireworks," he whispered back.

"So what was that noise?" Tango continued.

But before he could reply, Misty appeared. Her normally white front paws were covered in black wet mud, as was her muzzle.

Tango cocked her head.

"Rabbits," Misty said before Tango could ask.

"You're going to get into trouble," Tango replied.

Misty vigorously shook, sending mud all over Skipper's shiny red fur.

"Now you're in even bigger trouble," Tango added.

Skipper made no comment as he glanced at his half-sister and her muddy paws. Then he turned to Tango. "Why do you think Mom calls her 'The Devilish Miss M'?" he said, and sniffed Misty's white bib. "And that smell's not rabbit."

Misty's reply was a cheeky Corgi grin.

"What's going on?" Duke asked, appearing around a nearby bush. At six-years-old, he was the most senior of the siblings, but deferred to Skipper as the leader of their group.

"Fireworks," Tango replied.

"For the second time, that wasn't fireworks," Skipper snapped, but she ignored him and broke cover into the marshy field, immediately followed by Misty.

Skipper gave a low sharp bark that made them stop. "Get back here," he growled. "It's not safe. Time for breakfast."

At the word "breakfast," Tango turned back, but, as usual, Misty had to be told again, before she reluctantly followed.

The dogs entered the cottage-style house by way of a pet door to find their owner, mystery writer, Victoria 'Vicky' Cooper, in the newly remodeled kitchen, with four bowls already sitting on the counter.

"Perfect timing," she said, before noticing Misty's dirty face. "What did you do?" she added, already grabbing some paper towel.

"Stinky Miss M," Vicky continued, wiping the smelly mess off Misty's fur. "Phew! That's disgusting."

"See, I told you," Skipper said quietly to his siblings. "The devilish Miss M strikes again."

In typical Corgi fashion, their "breakfast" disappeared in record time.

After making sure their water bowl was full, Vicky picked up her mug of fresh coffee. "I'm going to write," she stated, before leaving the kitchen. "Behave yourselves."

As usual, Skipper immediately followed her, while the other three Corgis settled down for their morning nap.

"Peace at last," Duke muttered as he closed his eyes.

In Vicky's home office, Skipper settled at her feet, a regular routine since he was ten-weeks old. Back then, with no other siblings, he'd only interrupted Vicky's writing when he needed to go out, or be fed. And even when Misty arrived, a year later, he rarely left Vicky's side. Playtime with his new little half-sister was reserved until the evening, and didn't last very long, until Misty grew older. By then, Misty realized, that disturbing her owner at her computer was not a good idea. Duke, who was adopted from a previous owner, was already four years old when he met his sister and half-brother for the first time. Misty seemed to instinctively know that they were related, and she was even more delighted to finally have a full time playmate.

It wasn't until Vicky's third book made her famous, that the family moved to a new house in the small community of Cobbs Creek, Georgia. With her new-found fame, Vicky bought the rundown cottage, not only for its location, close to the marsh and water, but also for the peace and quiet. For the first time, the dogs had a large fenced garden in which to play, and although it first resembled an overgrown jungle, they made full use of it. But within weeks of moving in, the contractors arrived, and for the next nine months the house was full of workmen, tearing down walls and making a lot of noise in the general mess.

With Winter in coastal Georgia being very mild, to Skipper's relief, although he missed the snow, Vicky spent a great deal of that time working outside, also accompanied by Duke and Misty.

After a long weekend away at one of Vicky's book signings, to everyone's surprise, they returned home with a black and white Corgi puppy.

"This is Tango," Vicky told the dogs. "She's a tri-colored Corgi and your niece. So it's now Big Brother Skipper, Uncle Duke and Aunty Misty."

In the beginning, Tango was too young to be outside, so she spent a lot of time with the contractors. But as she grew up, Misty discovered that her niece not only hero-worshiped Skipper, but she also had exceptional digging skills. Consequently, it was Tango who mysteriously disappeared one morning, only to appear a few minutes later on the other side of the wooden split rail and wire mesh fence that surrounded the property.

"How did you do that?" Misty asked.

"I dug under the fence, behind that bush," Tango replied.

With Skipper being three times Tango's size, it took some more digging on Tango's part, before all four dogs had a hidden access to the marshy field and water channels beyond the garden. To date, their 'escape route' had yet to be discovered.

Vicky worked all day, and after feeding the dogs that night, she went back to her computer. Before following, Skipper crunched loudly on an ice cube, an after-dinner treat.

"What are we going to do about those humans we saw this morning?" Duke asked above the noise.

"Nothing we can do," Skipper replied.

"You could tell Mom," Misty said. "She listens to you."

Skipper finished his ice cube. "How? And if I do, our way to the marsh will be found out."

"Not necessarily," Tango said. "Take Mom to another part of the fence. She'll never know."

Skipper turned to go. "I'll think about it."

Tango watched him leave. "He'll come up with something, you'll see."

"Skipper, my hero," Misty mumbled, beginning to gnaw vigorously on a bone. "What do you think?" she added to Duke.

He put his head on a large and fluffy pink pig, a recent new toy. "I doubt that even he can pull this off," he said.

But little did Duke realize that he was about to be proved very wrong.

CHAPTER TWO

IT WAS THREE DAYS later, when Skipper started to bark. As he left all unnecessary barking to his siblings, Vicky knew immediately that someone was outside. A few seconds later, the doorbell rang.

She opened the front door to find Jake Robbins on the porch.

"Morning, ma'am," Jake said. "I hope it's not too early?"

"Not at all," Vicky replied. "Nice to see you again, Sheriff. Are you finally here for that rain check?"

Two days after the contractors began work, Jake had stopped at the cottage to welcome Vicky to the small community. But although she'd invited him inside, he could see all the chaos, and politely declined, saying, "I'll take a rain check, if that's okay with you?"

Now he could smell the fresh-brewed coffee as he followed Vicky into the kitchen.

"Smells good," he said, looking around. "You sure have done wonders with this place. But I'm really here on police business."

"That sounds serious," Vicky replied, handing him a mug of coffee.

He took a sip and shrugged. "Great coffee. But I was wondering if you've seen Bubba Smith lately?"

She shook her head. "I know he's my next door neighbor, but I only met him once, just after I moved in. That's not much help, is it?"

"It was a long shot, ma'am."

"It's Vicky, Sheriff."

He grinned. "Only if you call me Jake."

"Deal. So why are you looking for Mr. Smith?"

Jake cleared his throat. "He seems to have disappeared."

"That's terrible. When was this?"

"According to Ernie, the mail carrier, there's four days of mail in his box, and Bubba hasn't left town as far back as anyone can remember."

"There goes that theory," Vicky muttered.

"Tell her," Misty whispered. "I'll bet that was Bubba we saw."

"Patience," Skipper replied. "I'm thinking."

Jake bent down to stroke Skipper's head. "He sure is a good looking dog. Small, but very friendly."

"Not with everyone," Vicky said. "He likes you, and that's rare on a first meeting. He's very protective of his Mom."

"That's good," Jake replied. "Seeing as I didn't know we had a famous mystery writer in our community."

"I'm hardly famous."

"Not according to the locals. News tends to travel fast around here."

"You'd better act fast," Misty whispered again to Skipper.

Jake drained his coffee. "I've got to get going. Thanks for the coffee."

At that moment, Skipper gave a very sharp bark, getting everyone's attention.

"What's up?" Vicky asked him.

Skipper's reply was to bark again and do a quick pirouette, heading for the pet door. He repeated the maneuver several times, each time giving a short sharp bark.

"Looks like he's trying to get your attention," Jake commented.

"That's exactly what he's doing," Vicky said. "What is it?" she asked the dog.

Skipper's reply was to disappear through the pet door, giving another sharp bark on the other side.

"You'll have to excuse me," Vicky continued. "He really needs something."

Curious, and leaving the other Corgis inside, Jake decide to follow.

With Vicky and Jake now behind him, Skipper's odd behavior continued all the way to the fence.

"Now what?" Vicky asked, as they all came to a stop.

Skipper put his paws on the wire, and gave another short demanding bark.

"Guess he wants over," Jake said.

"But why? They've got a huge garden."

Jake climbed over the fence. "Hand him to me. Then we'll see."

"I don't think that's a good idea. He's really not good with strangers."

"Got a better idea?" Jake asked, and reached over the fence to tickle Skipper behind his ear. "I don't think he'll bite me."

Reluctantly, Vicky picked up Skipper and handed him to Jake.

No sooner was she also over the fence than Skipper gave another demanding bark and set off in the direction of the marsh.

"We get the picture," Jake said, running to keep up. "He sure seems to know where he's going."

"That's what worries me," Vicky replied, jogging some way back.

A dog's nose is hundreds of times more powerful than a human's, so it didn't take long for Skipper to find the spot where the dogs had seen the humans fighting in the fog.

He stopped just short of the area, and gave another sharp bark.

Jake was first to reach the spot, and at first he didn't see anything unusual. But Skipper began to dance again, making Jake get to his knees and look a lot more closely.

Just as Vicky reached them, Jake stood. "Don't come any closer," he ordered. "You've got one very smart dog. This looks like a possible crime scene."

Vicky's eyes widened. "You're serious?"

"Very," Jake replied.

Vicky turned to Skipper. "How did you know?"

Skipper gave her a big Corgi grin.

"You really are incredible," she added, giving him a big hug.

"I need gloves and my camera," Jake continued. "Can you stay, while I get them from my truck?"

"Of course," she replied. "You think something really happened here?"

"Looks that way. I won't be long." Jake pointed. "And stay away from that area."

An hour later, the area had been roped off with yellow crime scene tape stating; Police Line, Do Not Cross, and Jake was now accompanied by his young deputy, Hank Arnold.

"Didn't know we had a bloodhound in the department," Hank said at one point.

"We do now," Jake replied, stroking Skipper again.

"If you don't need me, I've got to get back to work," Vicky said.

"I could still use Skipper," Jake continued. "If that's okay with you?"

"If he'll stay with you, it's fine with me." Vicky cupped Skipper's face in her hands. "Jake needs your help again. So stay."

As she began to walk slowly away, Skipper was tempted to follow, but when he heard Jake say, "Come track, Skipper," he decided to remain with Jake.

Jake hadn't told Vicky that he'd found small traces of blood on blades of the long rough grass, and as soon as she was gone, he picked up a bullet casing with a gloved hand.

"This doesn't look good either," he said to Hank. Then he held the casing under Skipper's nose. "Follow," he added.

But Skipper didn't need the spent bullet casing to follow the trail. The faint whiff of blood was quite enough.

One hundred yards away, close to a tidal channel and hidden by palm branches and undergrowth at the base of an old Live Oak tree, Jake and Hank discovered that Bubba Smith was no longer missing.

Skipper sat some distance away, watching as the men carefully uncovered the body.

Jake finally straightened. "You know what to do," he said to Hank. "I've got to take the dog back to Miss Cooper."

"You think he saw what happened?" Hank asked.

"Yes. But don't ask me how. It's another mystery."

Back at the cottage, Misty and Tango could hardly contain their excitement, barking and rushing around in circles when Jake and Skipper returned.

"What did you find?"

"Why's the deputy here?"

"Tell us!"

"Tell us!"

"Enough, guys." Vicky ordered above the noise. "I can't hear myself think." She faced Jake. "Is everything okay?"

"Skipper found Bubba for us," he replied. "Unfortunately, he's dead. A homicide by the looks of it."

"Oh, no." Vicky quickly sat in the nearest chair. "That's terrible. Poor Mr. Smith."

As Skipper took a long drink from his water bowl, Duke turned to his sister and niece. "Now we know."

"Sorry, there was no easy way to say it," Jake continued to Vicky. "But I might need Skipper again. I'm thinking he was a witness."

"What about us?" Tango asked.

"Be quiet and listen," Duke replied. "You might just learn something."

"I don't know how he could be," Vicky replied. "You can't see that area he led us to from the garden."

"But he did know. He's got great instincts."

"We all have," Misty muttered. "How come no one's thanking us?"

"Sorry, I've got to go," Jake added. "I've got an investigation to begin."

"I quite understand," Vicky replied, walking him to the front door. "Please let me know if you find anything."

Jake turned. "This could turn out to be your next book."

She tried to smile. "I hope not."

The door closed.

Vicky leaned against it, her eyes closed. "What a strange morning." She then looked at all four dogs. "I've got no idea what you've been doing, but please stop. A murder? Whatever next?"

"This's so exciting," Tango said, as Vicky entered her office. "What do we do now? Can we go see?"

"No," Duke replied. "It's a miracle that they didn't find your hole. We don't go anywhere near it, until the humans have finished." He turned to Skipper. "Agreed?"

"Yes," Skipper said, cleaning his paws.

"We could sneak out," Misty said quietly to Tango. "No one would know."

"Yes, we would," Skipper replied. "And there's nothing wrong with my hearing. Understand?"

To Misty's and Tango's dismay, when the dogs were allowed out, later that day, Vicky came with them. At the fence where she'd lifted Skipper over, she stared into the distance, but there was no sign of anyone.

"Guess they've already finished," she said.

But back at the sheriff's department, Jake was only just beginning.

CHAPTER THREE

THE MAIN STREET OF Cobbs Creek was bathed in sunlight, but Jake didn't notice as he sat at his desk within the small Sheriff's Department building, and again studied the Medical Examiner's report on the death of Bubba Smith.

Earlier that morning, the old farmer's funeral was very well attended. The mourners included the mayor, most of the town's older residents, and Vicky Cooper.

"I wasn't expecting to see you here," Jake said, reaching her side as they left the churchyard.

All during the graveside service, he'd scanned the crowd in the hope that Bubba's killer might be there.

"You should have brought Skipper," he continued. "Seeing as he's my only probable witness."

Vicky stopped, adjusting her sunglasses. "That's the second time you've said that. I thought you were joking?"

"Not at all," Jake replied. "Like I said, he's a very smart dog."

"They all are." She hesitated. "Maybe you'd like to interview them, and then stay for dinner?"

Jake grinned. "Now that sounds like a plan."

Vicky was surprised. "It is? She thought quickly. "How about seven tonight?"

"I'll be there. Thanks."

She could hardly believe he'd accepted, and she was still smiling as she crossed Main Street at the only red light in town. Passing Jake's office on the corner, she continued down Marshside Road to the cottage.

He said yes to dinner, she thought. *Now I've got to think of something special.*

Two hours later, wearing shorts and a tank top, Vicky drove back to town. It never ceased to amaze her, as she turned onto Main

MAIN STREET

Street, that it looked like a set from a Disney movie. Most of the brightly painted store fronts were adorned with either hanging baskets of flowers, or large sidewalk planters, that were put out in April and didn't get removed until the middle of October. Then the street was decorated for Halloween, Thanksgiving, and finally, Christmas. That meant a lot of repeat business for Dolores Black, who owned the local garden center and flower shop. Tall, with jet black hair, usually worn in a ponytail, Dolores had a dazzling smile that could make even the darkest mood vanish. She was also a mine of information. Not used to living in such a small town, Vicky was amazed at the amount of gossip. If something was worth talking about, and even when it wasn't, Dolores seemed to be the informed source.

In keeping with their picture postcard image, Cobbs Creek had insisted that the modern supermarket chain was set back from the road, hidden behind a screen of trees and flowering bushes.

As much as Vicky wanted to stop and talk to Dolores about Jake, she didn't.

Some other time, she told herself as she shopped in record time, before driving home.

It was obvious to the dogs that Vicky was expecting someone for dinner. They kept a close watch on her as she marinated the steaks and set the table early.

"Who's coming?" Tango asked.

"Jake," Skipper replied.

"How do you know that?"

"Because they really like each other."

"This isn't good news," Duke said, when he hoped Skipper was out of earshot. "He thinks he's the only man in Mom's life."

"Maybe Jake will keep Mom occupied, so we can explore," Misty commented.

"You're such an opportunist," Duke continued.

"Well, someone has to be," Misty interrupted. "Otherwise, we'd never have any excitement."

"And that's just how I like it," Duke replied.

Jake arrived promptly at seven, carrying a bottle of wine and a bouquet of flowers.

"That's going to put the gossip mongers in high gear," Vicky said, seeing Dolores' flower shop label. "They're beautiful. Thank you."

Jake grinned. "It's the least I could do. And let them talk. They haven't had this much excitement since the mayor drove off the road one night, swerving to avoid a deer, and got stuck in a muddy pond for the night. The following morning, a local farmer found him sitting on the roof of his car. It took the volunteer fire department several hours to rescue him and the car. That kept the locals talking for weeks."

Vicky laughed. "That's really true?"

Jake grinned again. "Pretty much. Something smells good."

Yes, it does, the dogs thought in unison, following the couple into the kitchen.

But much to Misty's and Tango's disappointment, there was very little talk about Bubba Smith, and instead of being let out alone, both Vicky and Jake followed the dogs into the garden.

"So much for that idea," Duke said to his sister. "Better luck, next time."

"I'm not giving up."

"I didn't think for a moment you were," he replied.

Vicky and Jake stayed at the table long after dinner was over, the smell of barbecued steak still lingering in the dogs' nostrils. The chocolate dessert hadn't helped either.

It was almost midnight, when Jake took Vicky's hand at the front door.

"I had a really great evening," he said. "You're a great cook too." Then he kissed her on the cheek.

As far as Skipper was concerned, Jake had just gone too far. He barked loudly twice, and immediately moved to Vicky's side.

Jake took a step back. "Okay, Skipper," he said. "I get the picture. But your Mom's quite safe with me. "

"That's not the point," Skipper barked again.

"He really is protective," Jake continued. "I'd better say goodnight, before I lose some fingers or toes."

"I apologize," Vicky said. "But don't worry, he'll get used to you."

Don't bet on it, Skipper thought as the door closed, and they all heard Jake's SUV disappearing down the driveway.

CHAPTER FOUR

IT HAD BEEN ALMOST a month since Bubba Smith was murdered. Jake had become a regular dinner guest at the cottage, although Vicky finally stopped him from showing up with bouquets of flowers.

"It's very nice of you," she told him, "and they are beautiful, but the cottage is beginning to look like a funeral parlor."

Jake laughed. "Point taken."

But although the flowers had stopped, the town gossip steadily increased.

Now sitting at the table in the screen porch, the sunset long over, Vicky decided to comment on that fact.

Jake took a sip of beer. "They've got nothing better to do. Would you prefer that I stopped coming around?"

"No," she replied quickly. "I didn't mean that at all." *Time to change the subject*, she thought. "How's the investigation coming?"

She rarely asked, but this time made an exception.

Jake faced her across the table. "I was getting nowhere, until this afternoon," he said. "I got a call from Mike Burton, the local attorney, to say that he'd been contacted by a supposed distant relative of Bubba's, who was now in his office. So I told him, after he'd finished with him, to send him over to me."

Under the table, Tango nudged Misty. "This's so exciting."

"Shush," Misty whispered. "We might miss something."

"Did he come over?" Vicky asked.

"Sure did."

"And?" she added.

Jake cleared his throat. "I was wondering if I could borrow Skipper tomorrow?"

"You suspect this relative?"

"If that's who he really is. I've got nothing else."

"Will Mike Burton find out?"

"That's part of what lawyers do. And I could use a lead."

It was obvious to Vicky as Jake helped himself to another piece of peach pie, that this particular conversation was over.

As Jake was leaving, he stopped before opening the front door. "Is it okay if I pick up Skipper in the morning?"

"If you think it will help?"

"It's just a hunch."

With Vicky agreeing, Jake drove away.

"He doesn't strike me as the type to have hunches for no reason," she said to the dogs after Jake had gone. She bent down to stroke Skipper. "Help him out tomorrow. Who knows, this could well be the lead he's been looking for."

"This's so unfair," Tango whispered. "Skipper gets all the fun."

"I don't call coming face-to-face with a possible murderer, fun," Duke said. "You have a very strange sense of adventure."

"And you're an old party pooper," Misty replied to him.

"Less of the 'old,' please."

"You're all expecting too much," Skipper commented.

"But you will know, won't you?" Tango asked.

"Probably," Skipper said, following Vicky into the kitchen.

CHAPTER FIVE

"GOOD LOOKING POLICE DOG," Ernie, the mail carrier, commented to Jake the following morning. "A bit on the small side. I thought law enforcement used those German Shepards or Belgian Malinois?" He laughed. "Small town, small dog, eh, Sheriff?"

Jake stroked Skipper's head. "You can't judge a book by the cover, Ernie."

Ernie stared again at the dog, sitting quietly at the side of Jake's chair. "Now I know where I've seen him before. That's one of Miss Cooper's Corgis."

Ernie gave a broad grin. "Pet sitting is now part of the sheriff's department duties, is it?" he continued, before Jake could reply.

Jake kept a straight face. "No. He's a police dog in training. Later today, we're having a small ceremony to deputize him. He'll then have full police powers. So watch your speed in that mail truck of yours. He could give you a ticket."

Sitting at a desk across from Jake's, Hank managed to contain his laughter until after Ernie was back on the sidewalk.

"That news is going to get around town so fast, it would take Superman to catch it," he said.

"So let them talk. Seeing as we've got the lowest crime rate of anywhere in history, it gives them something to do," Jake replied.

"Unless you count a homicide."

"Yes, there is that."

"Do you think that Ralph Huggins will show?"

"That's why Skipper's here."

According to attorney Mike Burton, and Jake's own investigating, Ralph Huggins' claim of being Bubba Smith's cousin, twice removed, had, so far, proved to be legitimate.

"What's that mean, 'twice removed'?" Hank asked the previous day.

"It means that he's the great grandson of the sister or brother of Bubba's grandparents."

"That's why his name isn't Smith?"

"Correct."

Just as Jake was about to walk down the street to Polly Parker's deli and sandwich shop, the door to the sheriff's department opened, and a tall, skinny man entered.

Skipper, who had been dozing for most of the morning, was immediately wide awake, and to Jake's surprise, he gave a very low growl.

"Morning, Sheriff," Ralph Huggins said, and without being asked, sat on a chair across from Jake's desk. "I saw Attorney Burton again, this morning, and as far as he's concerned, I am who I say I am. Hope you checked me out, too? I'd really like to take possession of the farm."

He then peered around the corner of Jake's desk and gave a short laugh. "Funny looking police dog."

Jake didn't reply. He was more interested in watching Skipper's reaction.

Skipper stared back at the man called Huggins, whose dark hair was collar length and didn't appear to have been combed in days. His checked shirt was badly wrinkled, his jeans had several dark stains, and his boots were splattered in dried mud. But it wasn't how the man looked, or was dressed, that got his full attention. It was his smell.

Skipper's reply to an outstretch hand was to growl so quietly, only Jake heard it, but neither man mistook the risen hackles and a full mouth of very sharp, bared teeth. Skipper's large raised ruff made him look more like a small angry lion.

Huggins immediately withdrew his hand. "He's not very friendly."

"He's a trained police dog," Jake replied, recovering quickly, and noted Huggins' astonished look. "He may not be typical, but he's got some very unique skills."

Huggins edged his chair farther away. "So okay with you, if I move in?"

Jake thought quickly. "When all the legal work is complete, I don't have a problem." He sat more upright. "If you don't mind me saying, you seem in a bit of a hurry?"

Huggins fidgeted on the chair. "I'm, er, between homes, if you get my meaning?" he said slowly. "Losing a job can do that. You know how it is."

Jake didn't, but wasn't about to comment. "So where are you living now?"

"A cheap motel, this side of Atlanta."

Jake reached for a pad and pen. "Tell me again how you found out about Bubba's death?"

"Lucky coincidence, you could say, Sheriff," Huggins replied, and immediately noticed Jake's look. "I didn't mean it was luck that cousin Bubba was murdered," he quickly added.

"I hope not. Keep going."

As Jake took notes, Huggins told him that after losing his job in West Palm Beach, the money he'd manage to save hadn't lasted long. Having spent the last six months staying with various friends, he finally decided to look up the only relative he knew who was still living.

"...Imagine how I felt, when I got here and found out what had just happened," he ended.

Jake scanned his notes from the previous day. What Huggins had just told him was almost word for word, but Jake had found no reason, so far, not to believe him

He stood and held out his hand. "Welcome to the community, Mr. Huggins."

"Call me Ralph, Sheriff," Huggins said, returning the handshake. He peered around the desk again. "Nice to meet your dog, too."

Skipper's reply was another low growl.

"Even if he's not very friendly," Huggins added, making his way to the door.

Hank watched Huggins on the sidewalk, and then slowly saunter down the street, before he spoke.

"What do you make of that?" he asked, pointing at Skipper. "That was some reaction."

"Yes, it was," Jake replied. He stroked Skipper's head. "What do you know that I don't? I wish you could talk."

Me, too, Skipper thought.

"You believe Huggins' story?" Hank continued.

Jake shook his head. "No way. But I've also got no proof that he's lying. Neither has Mike Burton."

"Yet," Hank added. "Maybe the dog will find a way?"

"I sure hope so. Time to get some lunch?"

At the word 'lunch' Skipper sprang to his feet, heading for the door.

"Now don't tell me," Jake said, "that he doesn't understand every word we say."

"You'll get no argument from me," Hank replied, being to follow. "That's real weird. A bit scary, too."

With Skipper now on a leash, he waited at Jake's side outside the deli, as Hank ordered their sandwiches from Polly.

She gawked through the open doorway, grinning broadly. "Morning, Sheriff. Dog sittin' are we? You see that's what happens when you get a new lady friend."

Jake had already had enough. "Actually, he's a police dog in training," he said.

Polly couldn't tell if he was being serious or not. "You're kiddin' me?"

"Not at all, ma'am," Jake replied. "Even in a small town like ours, it's good to have extra backup. Especially after what happened to Bubba."

"So Miss Cooper's okay with you takin' him?"

"Of course. She's still got three. And deputy Skipper will take roast beef and cheese. Nothing more."

"Comin' right up, Sheriff," Polly replied.

That afternoon, the sheriff's department became a revolving door for the local residents, whose excuses for being there ranged from complaining about shoddy garbage collection, noisy roosters, fighting cats, and dogs not being leashed, to actually being truthful about their curiosity in seeing the new police dog.

"You've really opened a can of worms," Hank said, as Jake locked the door at 5:30 p.m. "I've never seen so many people in here in one day. I don't know what you're going to tell Miss Cooper. That's if she doesn't already know that you've kidnapped her dog."

Jake shook his head. "I'm an idiot. I never thought it would go this far."

Hank grinned. "I'd like to be a fly on the wall when you try and explain it to her. In the meantime, you'd better think seriously about deputizing him. Otherwise, we're both going to be a laughing stock."

"And you don't think we already are?"

"No. I think the locals believe you."

Jake opened the door to the white Sheriff's Department SUV, allowing Skipper to jump in and sit on the passenger seat.

"See," Hank added. "He's right at home. You take care of the sheriff," he added to the dog.

"You told them what!" Vicky exclaimed, after Jake tried to explain.

"It's just for a few days," he replied.

"You expect me to just hand Skipper over to you? No, you've gone too far."

"I'll pick him up in the morning and bring him back at night. He'll be quite safe."

"He'd better be. And as far as agreeing, I'm going to let him decide."

"You have a deal. He ate lunch."

"What kind of lunch?"

"Roast beef and cheese."

Vicky finally smiled. "Fine. But from now on, he only eats here. He'll be overweight in no time."

"Police work can be very demanding."

"So I understand. Deputy Skipper Cooper?"

"That's right."

"This is definitely another book. And you make sure he's never off his leash."

"Tell us! Tell us!" Tango demanded when the dogs were finally alone.

"It was Ralph Huggins," Skipper replied. "He was the man we saw with Bubba Smith. I could smell him."

"Does Jake know?" Misty asked.

"I think he knows something isn't right when I growled and showed my teeth."

"You're going to have to do a lot better than that," Duke commented. "Otherwise, you'll just get a bigger reputation for being difficult with strangers."

"I'm not difficult," Skipper said. "I like to be quite sure before I trust someone."

"It's called difficult," Duke repeated.

Skipper glared.

"Ignore my brother," Misty said quickly. "He can be just as stubborn as the rest of us."

"And you should know," Duke replied.

Skipper took Misty's advice and went to find Vicky and Jake.

"A police dog?" Duke continued when he was sure Skipper couldn't hear. "That's going to make his head so big it wouldn't fit through a doorway."

"I think it's just perfect," Tango said. "He'll be so good at it."

"Yes, you would think that," Duke added, finally walking away to find his fluffy pink pig.

Chapter Six

At 8:30 a.m., with Skipper on a leash, Jake rounded the corner from his official Sheriff's Department parking space to find John Mayhew waiting, camera in hand.

"Hold it right there, Sheriff," Mayhew said, taking a second photograph. "That's just perfect. So this is the new police dog?" He stepped forward in an attempt to stroke Skipper.

"Don't," Jake ordered, immediately shortening Skipper's leash, and very grateful that only minutes earlier, he'd clipped an old deputy's badge to Skipper's collar, with the words, "Consider yourself deputized, Skipper."

"He's a police dog," Jake now continued. "Not some family pet."

"Right," Mayhew replied, taking several steps back. "Bite will he?"

"I doubt you'd want to find out."

"I'm sure you're right, Sheriff," Mayhew continued, staying back as Jake unlocked the office door. "I'd like to make him the lead story in this week's paper," he added, beginning to follow Jake inside.

As Jake took his seat, and without any command, Skipper immediately sat beside the desk.

Jake un-clipped his leash. "Why would you want to do that?"

Mayhew continued to stand. "It's big news. All over town. I'd hoped you'd give me some inside information? He's very well behaved."

"Police dogs are well trained."

"And expensive, from what I've learned?"

"Not always."

Mayhew finally sat, a notebook in one hand, a pen in the other. "I'm told that Miss Cooper gave him to you?"

"No. He's on loan to the sheriff's department."

"That's very unusual, isn't it? Don't police dogs have to go through many months of special training?"

"The less intelligent ones do, yes."

"So apart from being small, and just a loan, he's smart?"

Jake nodded. "Ask him something."

"Like what?" Mayhew asked.

"You're the reporter. Isn't it your job to ask questions?"

After a hesitation, Mayhew cleared his throat and looked reluctantly into a pair of dark brown eyes. "Do you like being a police dog?"

Skipper barked once.

"He said, yes," Jake translated.

When Mayhew left the office, fifteen minutes later, he was still shaking his head in amazement.

"By the way," Jake said, as Mayhew opened the door. "Skipper's grandfather belongs to Queen Elizabeth II. So he really is a royal Corgi, but there's no need to call him 'sir.' Deputy Skipper will do just fine."

"Thanks," Mayhew replied, making his escape, just as Hank came into view.

"Got a call from the Jenkins about a prowler over at Bubba Smith's old place," Hank said before Jake could ask. "I went to check it out. It was Huggins, beginning to move in." He turned to watch Mayhew cross Main Street some way down. "What did he want?"

"We're his lead story."

"Then let's hope the Chief doesn't find out. If he does, you'll have some explaining to do," Hank continued, beginning to make a pot of coffee. "I'm surprised you didn't make this, already?"

"I didn't want to give Mayhew any reason to stay any longer," Jake said. "So Huggins is moving in?"

"Got a truck with some appliances and boxes," Hank replied. "He must have got it out of storage."

"He told you that?"

"No, I just assumed."

"Never, never do that," Jake ordered. "I think later today, deputy Skipper and I will pay him a visit."

"His badge looks good. I guess it really was okay with Miss Cooper then?"

"I wouldn't go quite that far," Jake replied. "But for now, he'll be working with us."

Later that morning, Jake and Skipper strolled down Main Street. They were stopped every few paces by curious residents, and even some tourists with cameras.

From his newspaper office above the hardware store, Mayhew watched from his window. When he finished university, with a degree in journalism, he'd had much bigger plans than to return to a backwater like Cobbs Creek and take over his father's weekly newspaper. But shortly before graduation, his father became seriously ill. After making him a promise to keep the paper going, Mayhew had every intention of either selling it, or just closing it down after his father's death. But he soon found out that a small town newspaper kept him very busy. The fact that he was the owner, editor, and the only reporter, didn't help. After ten years, all thoughts of his big-time journalism career had all but vanished. Until now. Watching the young local sheriff with the equally young Corgi, and the crowd they attracted, made him realize that they could well be his ticket to the big leagues. Reluctantly, he turned away from his window, but he was smiling as he picked up the telephone.

Skipper tried to ignore the comments of "He's so small," and concentrated on remarks like "He's gorgeous" "He's so handsome," and "You can tell by just looking at him that he's very intelligent."

Jake kept replying, "Thanks, I think so too," and "Yes, he is."

Every time Jake stopped, Skipper sat.

"Enough of this," Jake finally said. "I bet you're getting as fed up as I am?"

Skipper gave a low bark. *But I don't mind all the compliments*, he thought.

"Okay, lunch it is. Then a trip to see Huggins. You don't like him, do you?"

Skipper gave another short bark. *No, I don't.*

"Me neither," Jake added, heading toward the SUV.

He called Hank on the radio. "Skipper and I are going out to the farm. Hold the fort."

"Ten-four," Hank replied.

But on his way out of town, Jake stopped at the supermarket. Parking the SUV in the shade, with the windows down, he told Skipper to stay and guard. Then he crossed the parking lot to get a sandwich at the deli counter.

From his view through the windshield, Skipper saw Jake go inside the supermarket, and was about to settle on the seat, when he saw an old red pickup enter the parking lot. As it got closer, he could see Huggins behind the wheel.

Huggins parked, three cars away, and was so busy talking on a cell phone that he failed to notice the white Sheriff's Department SUV.

When he did get out of the pickup, Skipper didn't realize that he'd barked so loudly, it made Huggins stop and turn. Then he slowly approached the passenger side window. Skipper knew that if he jumped through the open window, he'd probably break a leg in the long drop, or worse, so he put his paws over the door, and snarled at Huggins, his hackles raised to their full extent. When Huggins realized that the window was open, he stopped short.

"I'll get you, you mangy excuse for a real dog," he hissed, his voice angry and low. "Your days are numbered. Mark my words."

Before Skipper flew at him, regardless of the risk, they both heard Jake's voice. "Can I help you, Ralph?"

He turned. "Just saying hello to your dog. He's one fine animal."

"Thanks," Jake replied. "I think so. Glad I caught you. I had planned on stopping at the farm, this afternoon."

"You're welcome any time, Sheriff. I'm just stocking up on a few supplies. See you later then?"

"A hour okay?"

"No problem."

Jake then noticed the pickup. "That's Bubba's old truck, isn't it?"

Huggins nodded. "I had to buy a new battery to get it started, but at least I've got a set of wheels. Even if they aren't very pretty."

"This afternoon, then," Jake said, effectively ending the conversation.

As he stroked the still raised hackles, Jake knew immediately how angry Skipper was.

"I know he's a bad guy," he continued, still watching Huggins cross the parking lot and talking again on a cell phone. "And together we'll prove it."

Skipper licked his hand.

"Look," Jake added, "I know your Mom said 'no lunch,' but how about some sliced chicken breast?"

Skipper's answer was to demolish the chicken in two quick gulps.

"Just as I thought," Jake said, beginning to munch on a sandwich.

When Huggins left the supermarket, twenty-five minutes later, he was pushing a cart loaded with groceries, and still talking on his cell phone. To his relief, the white SUV was gone.

"No, he's not here," Huggins said to the person on the other end. "Stop worrying. A small time, nosy sheriff and his wretched little dog aren't going to be a problem. Trust me on this."

But little did Huggins know that he was being watched by two pairs of eyes from within the SUV, now hidden from view by bushes and a delivery truck at the side of the building.

"For a guy with no money, that looked like at least two hundred dollars worth of groceries. Agree?"

Skipper gave a short bark.

Jake tickled him behind an ear. "Before we officially go snooping, there's something I've got to do. Okay with you?"

If I knew what is was, I could comment, Skipper thought.

But he soon found out.

At the local school playing field, Jake stopped the SUV and let Skipper out. Then removing his leash, he gave him a series of commands. "Sit." "Stay." "Heel." Skipper knew them all and obeyed perfectly.

At the command, "Stay and guard," Jake left Skipper by the side of the SUV and walked the length of the field. When he did eventually turn around, he was delighted to see the dog hadn't moved.

"Skipper come!" he shouted.

In an instant, the Corgi was flying toward him, at a speed that even surprised Jake.

"You're really fast," he said as Skipper skidded to a halt and sat. "Good boy. I've got to start carrying treats."

Yes, you have, Skipper thought.

The old farm gate, leading to Huggins' newly inherited farm, hadn't been closed in years. It was partly off its large hinges and half-buried by tall weeds. The driveway to the farmhouse was no more than a rutted track, with grass and weeds down the center, and broken down fences on either side. When Bubba's father bought the farm, long before he was born, and in Bubba's younger days, it had been very well cared for and profitable. But Bubba never married, and as he grew older, he sold the dairy cows and stopped cutting the hay. The fields soon went back to part wilderness, and the house was no better. Unable or unwilling to afford the new roof it desperately needed, Bubba had spent the last twenty years, living on first floor to avoid getting wet whenever it rained.

Jake had intended using the front door, but there was no sign of the red pickup outside the farmhouse. On Jake's occasional visits to check up on the elderly farmer, before his untimely end, Bubba had shown him old photographs of what the house originally looked like. Jake's only thought, as he now viewed the jungle, was that Bubba's mother was probably turning over in her grave at the sight of such neglect. The manicured lawns and huge flower beds were long gone, as was the large vegetable garden to the left of the house. And what remained of the orchard, Jake thought, was probably not worth saving. Bubba's mother had not only grown enough food for the family, but also plenty more for her stall at the weekly farmer's market. She was famous for her fruit and vegetables, as well as, her bunches of fresh-cut flowers.

Jake drove around the back, parking in a large courtyard formed by the house, and equally dilapidated milking shed and large old barn.

Huggins was in the process of unloading the pickup as Jake approached.

"Just in time," Huggins said. "Grab some bags, Sheriff. There's some beer somewhere."

With the command, "Stay," Jake left Skipper by the side of the SUV and followed Huggins toward the house.

"You can bring your dog inside," Huggins said.

"No, thanks," Jake replied. "He's used to being outside."

No, I'm not, Skipper thought, watching the men disappear.

Jake wasn't about to admit, from his few previous visits to the farm, that he knew the inside of the house was in no better shape than the exterior. Vicky would probably never speak to him again, if she ever found out that Skipper had been exposed to so many bugs and dirt.

But he was surprised, on entering the kitchen, that Huggins had obviously been very busy. A large, new stainless steel refrigerator was already plugged in, as was an equally new stove and microwave. The old planked floors had been swept and washed, as had the few cabinets.

"Can't believe my cousin lived like this," Huggins said, trying to hand Jake a beer.

He made no comment. "No, thanks. I'm on duty," he said instead.

"Coffee then?" Huggins asked. "The coffee maker's new, too."

"I can see that. You've been busy."

"Got a long way to go. I've seen pigs live better. But the place has got potential."

Jake immediately thought of Vicky's cottage. "It didn't always look like this. You've probably seen the old photographs?"

"Not yet," Huggins replied. "There's a lot of stuff to go through. So this is a social call, Sheriff?"

"Partly," Jake replied. "I still have an on-going investigation into your cousin's murder. And I want you to know that I won't rest until the individual or individuals responsible are caught. Then punished to the full extent of the law."

Huggins forced a smile. "Well it's nice to know that you're so dedicated."

"It's my job, Ralph."

Skipper waited by the SUV for a couple of minutes. In his mind, it was long enough. Then he padded quietly across the weedy courtyard, heading for the old milking shed. Inside, his first thought was that Misty and Tango would be salivating at all the smells, and possible games they could play, chasing all the shed's furry inhabitants.

A large brown rat peeked out from a hole, while overhead, Skipper knew he was being watched by several squirrels and some birds. He had to stop himself from barking a warning, but the animals and birds seemed to sense he wasn't their friend, and either flew or scuttled quickly away.

Apart from all the smells, there was nothing more of interest in the shed, so he left, squeezing through a gap in the old double doors of the barn. At first, all he saw was an old rusty tractor,

THE OLD BARN

an equally rusty plow, a broken down lawn mower and lots of rusty tools hanging from nails in the thick wood-planked walls. But his nose told him that Huggins and maybe two other humans had spent time in there, and recently, too. Their trail coincided with the covering of rotting straw on the old dirt floor that looked like something had been dragged across it. It ended at a tall stack of rotting hay bales that reached almost to the partially collapsed floor of the loft in the high ceiling.

Skipper studied the hay bales in front of him and the old wooden loft ladder, knowing that there was no way he was going to be able to climb them. He'd overheard Mom joke that Corgis had the blood of Mountain Goat in their veins. Not only would they eat almost anything, but they also loved to climb. Skipper wished it was true as he paced up and down the stack, trying to find a place to squeeze through. When he didn't find one, he trotted outside and around the rear of the barn.

As he hoped, some of the large planks closest to the ground were beginning to rot, and although there were some large holes, none of them were big enough for him to get through.

I need Tango, he thought. *There's something strange behind those hay bales, but I don't know what.*

"Skipper! Here boy! Skipper!"

He turned and flew around the barn to see Jake by the SUV, with Huggins at his side.

As he reached them, Jake opened the door, and without a hesitation, Skipper jumped for the passenger seat.

"I expect he was just being a dog," Jake said. "Lot's of new smells to explore."

"Expect you're right," Huggins replied. Then he glared at Skipper, leaving him in no doubt as to what Huggins really thought.

Jake didn't see the exchange, as he put the SUV in gear, and drove away.

As he reached the end of the rutted driveway, he called Hank.

"I know the guy is dirty," Jake said "At one point, he rolled up his sleeves and I saw a prison tattoo. Plus Skipper went exploring the outside barns. I'm sure he found something."

"Did he tell you what?" Hank asked.

"Don't be stupid," Jake replied. "I need you to start digging into Huggins' background. I'm taking Skipper home."

Back at the cottage, Skipper was greeted by his siblings with their usual enthusiasm.

"What happened?" "Tell us!" they kept repeating.

"You're back early," Vicky said to Jake. "Is everything okay?"

"It's fine," he replied. "Skipper and I had a busy day. As I've got a lot of paperwork to do, I thought I'd better bring him back now, rather than later." He stroked Skipper's head. "Good job today. Thanks."

Vicky eyed them both with suspicion. "You're quite sure there's nothing I should know?"

Jake nodded. "Sure. I'll see you in the morning."

As the SUV left the driveway, she looked down at Skipper. "And I know you're not going to tell me, even if you could."

After taking a drink form the water bowl, Skipper flew through the pet door, followed immediately by his siblings.

"Where's the fire?" Duke asked outside.

"No fire," Skipper replied. "But I needed to get you away from Mom."

"Something happened, didn't it?" Tango asked, and before Skipper could reply, she continued, "I knew it! I just knew it!"

Misty couldn't contain her excitement, and began to run in circles. "Tell us! Tell us now!"

"He will, if you shut up," Duke said. "Continue like that, and Mom will be out here."

Misty immediately stopped.

"There was a man waiting for us this morning..." Skipper began.

"... so we have to find way to get Tango to the barn," he finished, sometime later.

"That's easy," Duke said. "With you now gone all day, Mom's been letting us into the garden without her."

Skipper faced him. "I didn't know that."

"Regardless of what Tango thinks, you don't know everything," Duke replied.

"Enough," Misty barked. "We need a plan."

"Whatever you decide, I think it's a very bad idea," Duke continued.

"Yes, you would," his sister muttered.

Duke stopped to watch a large colorful butterfly land on a flowering bush. "If you go all the way to the farm, Mom won't be there to help, if anything goes wrong."

"Then Misty and I will go alone," Tango said.

Misty grinned. "Perfect. Why didn't I think of that."

"Because you're expected to have at least some commonsense," Duke commented.

Tango reached Skipper's side. "Don't worry. I'll get into the barn for you."

"Duke's right," Skipper said. "Be very careful."

Tango suddenly saw a squirrel. "I will!" she barked, as she raced down the lawn in hot pursuit.

Chapter Seven

Jake wasn't the only one having a very bad morning.

It had been two days since he and Skipper had been confronted by Mayhew, outside the sheriff's office, and to his short lived relief, when he went to collect Skipper, earlier that morning, Vicky had yet to open the local paper.

"Your Mom's really mad with me," Jake said now to Skipper, as he replaced the receiver. "She's just seen the photograph and article about us in the newspaper. She's so mad, she thinks I should take you home, right now."

"The mayor's on line one," Hank interrupted.

"Tell him, I'm busy."

"I don't think that's going to work."

"Great photograph and article," the mayor said, as Jake reluctantly took his call. "It's really going to put Cobbs Creek on the map. That means a lot more tourist dollars. Well done."

It was not at all what Jake was expecting, and all he could say was, "Thank you, Mr. Mayor."

After Vicky finished her angry call to Jake, she then called Mayhew.

"Thanks very much!" she snapped. "How dare you print that story without my permission. If your article puts Skipper in any danger, I'll hold you personally responsible. And that's no idle threat. I moved here for peace and quiet. You've now ruined that. Call yourself a newspaper man? Where are your ethics?"

Mayhew, with what he had planned, quickly decided that the best course of action was to apologize, but Vicky was in no mood to listen.

I'll do it without her, he thought, after she hung up.

His telephone rang again.

"I hope you realize that you've just made the dog a target?" Jake almost shouted. "If the killer or killers read that article of yours, they'll know I think he was a witness. So from now on, don't expect anymore cooperation from me, or the sheriff's department. Is that clear?"

The line went dead before Mayhew could reply.

It's only a dog, he thought. *It's not like he's going to tell anyone if he really did see the murder. How dumb is that?*

Vicky paced the kitchen, watched closely by Duke, Misty and Tango.

"How could he?" she said aloud. "How could Jake agree do that without telling me." She turned to the dogs. "It's okay, guys. Mommy's not mad at you."

"But she sure is mad at Jake," Duke whispered.

"What did he do?" Tango asked.

"I don't know."

"It's something to do with the newspaper," Misty said. "I wonder what?"

"Skipper will tell us, when he gets home," Tango replied.

Duke glanced across at his niece. "If he knows."

"Of course, he knows," Tango added.

"He we go again," Duke muttered.

By mid-morning, the sheriff's department telephone was still ringing off the hook. Most of the calls were from local residents congratulating Jake, not only for an interesting article, but also for a great photograph. Some even wanted him to autograph it.

"I've had enough," he finally said, after replacing the receiver from the latest call. "Come on Skipper. We're leaving."

Skipper didn't need to be told twice, and was already waiting at the door as Jake got to his feet.

"Unless it's an emergency, you don't know where I am," he instructed Hank, before closing the door behind them.

Skipper was expecting their usual walk down Main Street, but instead, Jake headed directly to the SUV.

"Let's go play," he said, backing out of his parking space. "And this time, I've got treats."

Good deal, Skipper thought.

Sitting at the old pine table in the farmhouse kitchen, Huggins read the newspaper article for the third time.

I knew it, he thought. *That wretched little dog did see something. Time for plan B. And then we'll see just how smart you think you are.*

As far as Duke, Misty and Tango were concerned, whatever had happened that morning to put their Mom in such a bad mood, was actually good news for them.

Without giving it much thought, she let them out, before going directly to her computer to write a nasty letter to the editor of the Cobbs Creek Times.

"Free at last!" Tango barked.

"Yippee!" Misty replied.

"Behave yourselves," Duke ordered. "If we upset Mom anymore, we'll all pay the price."

"He's no fun," Misty said quietly.

Tango grinned. "Ignore him. I've got a plan."

"What?" Misty asked.

"Just follow my lead," Tango replied.

The dogs spent several minutes sniffing around the bushes, when suddenly Tango took off at a high rate of speed down the lawn.

"Squirrels!" she barked, as Misty gave chase.

Duke turned, watching the two of them disappear out of sight behind the bushes.

"What squirrels? I don't see any squirrels. They're both nuts."

Tango squeezed through the hole under the fence, with Misty close behind.

"Have we lost him?" she asked.

Misty looked back. "Duke's not stupid," she replied. "He'll soon find us."

"Then we'd better hurry," Tango continued, beginning to cross the marsh.

Much to their relief, the shortest route to the farmhouse and barn took them away from the area where they had seen the two humans fighting.

Corgis have a reputation of having a foxy nature that matches their foxy looking faces, and in this particular case, Misty and Tango's natural instincts were being put to good use. They crossed the marsh in record time, keeping low, and avoiding the worst of the wet ground.

Twenty feet from the rear of the barn, the rusty barbed wire fence was no problem, as they wriggled under the lowest strand of wire, careful not to get snagged. Then they quickly and quietly made their way through the weedy open area, before reaching the planked barn wall.

"I see what Skipper means," Misty commented, eyeing the holes. "There's no way he could squeeze through those. I doubt even I can."

"I'm small enough," Tango replied.

"Yes, you are. But please be careful?"

"I will," Tango continued, choosing the biggest hole.

Her head went through easily, but her shoulders were still too wide. Not wanting to give up, she wiggled and pushed, and pushed and wiggled, until some of the rotting wood finally gave way, and she was inside the barn.

"What can you see?" Misty asked, putting her head through the now enlarged hole.

"Lots of boxes," Tango replied from somewhere inside. "They've got a funny smell."

"What kind of smell?"

"I don't know. It's not like anything I've smelled before."

"What do you think you're doing?" Duke hissed, making Misty jump. "Where's Tango?"

Misty backed up and faced her brother. "In there," she said. "What are you doing here?"

"Trying to make sure you don't get into too much trouble." He tried unsuccessfully to look inside the darkened barn. "Tango, get out of there, right now."

A moment later, Tango's head appeared, and with some more pushing and wriggling, she was soon back in the sunlight.

"What's that smell?" she asked Duke as he stepped forward and was now able, thanks to Tango's efforts, to stick his head through the hole.

There was a long pause. "I don't know," he finally said, removing his head. "But I do know, we've been here long enough. I can smell humans. Where's Tango?"

Misty looked around. "I don't know. She was right here."

"Then find her," Duke ordered.

Keeping close to the rear of the barn, both dogs carefully rounded the far corner, to see, ahead of them, Tango peering into the courtyard.

"Get back here, now!" Duke snapped. "You really are crazy."

"There's no one home," Tango said. "The truck's not here."

"Maybe he keeps it in the garage, like Mom does," Duke continued. "Did you think of that?"

Before Tango could reply, they all heard the familiar sound of an engine, and it was getting louder.

"Time to go," Duke hissed. "Now!"

Still young and very athletic, so much so, that the dogs had all overheard Vicky talk about training Tango, when she got older, for agility trials, she was under the barbed wire way ahead of her aunt and uncle, and took off across the marsh so fast, that Duke and Misty had trouble keeping up.

They didn't stop until they reached the safety of the trees and undergrowth.

"That was way too close," Duke said. "It's a very good thing we weren't seen."

Huggins wasn't sure as the pickup entered the courtyard, but, with the sun behind his back, he thought he'd just caught sight of some dogs, running through the marsh.

One way to check, he said to himself, walking slowly around the barn.

When he didn't find anything, he was about to leave, when he looked down. Caught on some freshly broken rotting wood were small traces of silky black fur. When he studied the enlarged hole more closely, he also found strands of red fur.

He straightened, looking across the now empty marsh.

"Pesky little varmints." Then he gave a cruel smile. "Your days are definitely numbered. So if you ever come back, you're going to get a very unpleasant surprise."

He turned back to the barn, and decided that it wasn't worth the effort to nail a plank of wood to cover the hole.

Vicky was waiting in the driveway as Jake's SUV came to a stop.

"I'm sorry…" he began, handing her Skipper's leash.

"Don't," she interrupted. "Nothing you can say is going to help. As far as I'm concerned, this is over. From now on,

Skipper stays with me. So don't bother coming to get him. Do you understand?"

He nodded.

"Good," she continued, turning on her heel. "Come on, sweetheart," she added to Skipper. "Time to go inside."

Vicky never looked back as the front door closed, leaving Jake in the driveway.

Skipper got the usual enthusiastic greeting from his siblings, but, as it was obvious that Vicky wasn't in the best of moods, the dogs waited until after dinner to exchange stories. Vicky returned to her computer, leaving the dogs alone, and this time, Skipper didn't go with her.

By now, Tango could hardly contain herself. "I got into the barn. I did. I did!"

"And that nasty man Huggins almost saw us," Misty added.

"Where were you?" Skipper asked Duke.

"Trying to make sure they didn't get caught."

After listening to the whole story, Skipper then told them about his day with Jake. After a lot of discussion, they finally decided that they should return to the barn, to help out Jake. When, none of them yet knew.

Chapter Eight

THE SHERIFF'S DEPARTMENT DIDN'T close just because it was the weekend. But with no Skipper to pick up, and a growing pile of paperwork to go through, Jake had been at his desk even earlier than usual.

The coffee pot was already half empty, when loud voices from outside interrupted him at 9:00 a.m. Through the windows, he saw a white TV station van, with its call sign painted in large letters on the side.

He was about to get to his feet, when the door opened and a well-dressed young woman entered, followed by a video cameraman wearing shorts and a tee shirt, with the TV station logo printed on the front.

"Sheriff Robbins," she said with a bright white smile and immediately stuck a microphone between them, signaling frantically with her other hand for the cameraman to start taping. "Please tell the viewers of WQRXTV how a small dog became your only witness in a…" She didn't have time to complete the sentence as Jake made a grab for the microphone.

"Turn that off," he ordered the cameraman, coming around the desk. "No interviews, on or off the record," he added. "Is that clear?"

The cameraman took several hasty steps backward.

"Oh, come now, Sheriff," the woman continued. "Sorry if we got off to a bad start. I'm Jenny Beale, the news anchor of..."

"I know who you are," Jake interrupted again, hoping that her thickly applied makeup and black false eyelashes were meant for a TV studio. "There's no story for you here."

"You're so wrong," she said quickly.

Jake took another step toward her. "No, I'm not. You're interfering with police business, and possibly putting lives in danger. So leave, before I confiscate the camera, and place you under arrest for trespassing."

The cameraman didn't need to be told twice, and made a hasty exit, while the argument within the office continued for several more minutes, clearly overheard by those on the sidewalk.

Jenny was still trying to get back her composure, as she rejoined her cameraman.

"That wasn't good," he said.

"Some small town sheriff isn't going to stop me," she hissed. "Let's start interviewing the residents. You know how the public love seeing themselves on television."

"Then you'd better start with John Mayhew," the cameraman said. "Seeing as he gave you the story."

The deal Mayhew had put together with Jenny Beale, earlier in the week, was that he get full credit for her exclusive, or he'd give the story to another network. And he wanted the agreement in writing to make sure that she didn't double-cross him.

Jenny soon discovered that Mayhew was actually very good on camera. Surprisingly so.

"He's a natural," she whispered to the cameraman at one point.

By the time the day was half over, even the mayor had been interviewed.

Jenny's visit to Polly Parker's deli, to get an lunchtime sandwich, had lasted almost two hours, as information about the sheriff and mystery writer, Vicky Cooper, owner of the dog in question, continued to grow. Jenny also got Vicky's address.

At 3:00 p.m., she rang the front door bell to Vicky's cottage, but long before the door opened, Jenny could hear dogs barking.

"Get ready," she told the cameraman.

Vicky opened the door.

"And this," Jenny began to the camera, before quickly turning back to Vicky, "is famous mystery writer, Victoria Cooper." She then thrust a microphone under her nose.

"Get off my property," Vicky replied. "And turn that off. I'm not giving an interview to you, or anyone."

Jenny signaled to the cameraman, and the video camera stopped recording. She gave Vicky a huge smile. "So sorry to take you by surprise, like this, Miss Cooper. My fault entirely. We were hoping that we could spend a few minutes with you and your beautiful dogs. This's such a great story. "

"To you, maybe," Vicky replied. "But not to me. I will not have them put in any danger by some two-bit TV reporter. Is that clear? Now leave, before I call the sheriff."

Jenny held her anger in check at being called a 'two-bit reporter,' although she'd been called worse. She tried again. "Could we at least get some tape of the dogs?"

"What is it about the word 'no,' you don't understand?" Vicky asked. "I would have thought that you would have better things to do than invade people's privacy? If you want to help catch a murderer, perhaps you should be keeping quiet about a police investigation, instead of broadcasting all the details."

Jenny was about to reply, when the loud noise of four Corgis barking again signaled Jake's SUV skidding to a halt in the driveway.

He could tell immediately from Vicky's expression what she thought of Jenny Beale and her cameraman.

"You need to leave," he told them. "The threat of arrest is looming larger. Got that?"

Reluctantly, Jenny turned away, heading for the TV van.

"We've got enough," she whispered to the cameraman. "The rest, we'll make up."

Jake watched as the van left, before he faced Vicky. "I'll make sure they don't bother you again."

"Thank you," she replied, and opened the door. Ever the opportunist, Skipper rushed passed her, greeting Jake in the driveway like a long lost friend, while Vicky watched.

She hesitated. "Do you have time for tea?"

"Thanks. Tea sounds good."

In the kitchen, she placed a tall glass in front of him. "I think I might have overacted. I owe you an apology."

"No, you don't," Jake said. "I was assuming too much."

She smiled. "I never asked Skipper what he wanted," she continued. "He sat by the door, all morning, refusing to move. He was expecting you."

"See, I said it would work," Skipper whispered to his siblings.

"He did?" Jake asked.

Vicky nodded. "So if you want to take him, it's okay with me. But please make sure nothing happens to him?"

"It won't," he replied. "And thank you to agreeing."

"Have we seen the last of that dreadful Beale woman?"

"I hope so," Jake continued. "But don't watch the news tonight. There's nothing I can do about that."

But they did watch the news. Together. Not sure that Jenny Beale had taken his threat seriously, Jake readily agreed to Vicky's invitation to stay to dinner.

"Back to normal," Misty commented from under the table.

"Don't be so sure," Skipper replied, just as the music introducing the six o'clock news began.

Jenny appeared behind a desk, smiling sweetly at the camera.

"Tonight's top story is that of famous mystery writer Victoria Cooper's Welsh Pembroke Corgis. One of her dogs is thought to be a witness to the murder of Bubba Smith in Cobbs Creek, last month…" she began.

"Oh, no," Vicky muttered.

"Damn her," Jake said.

"At least she got our breed correct," Skipper whispered.

"We saw too," Tango replied. "Why's everyone ignoring that?"

"Shuuuuuush," Skipper added. "We'll miss what she says."

"He just wants to be a star," Duke mumbled.

"No, I don't."

To Jake and Vicky's increasing horror, Jenny Beale was making good use of all the videotape that had been taken of the local residents. Mayor Cobb, after whose ancestors the town was named, appeared smiling on the screen, and talked at length about having a celebrity living in their midst. At that point, Vicky closed her eyes. There was a lot of footage of Main Street, interviews with Polly Parker, Dolores Black, several other residents, and even Ernie, the mail carrier.

"They're lovely dogs," Ernie said. "Very friendly and smart. I always look forward to delivering Miss Cooper's mail."

But the longest interview, by far, was with John Mayhew.

The story finally ended.

"Mayhew looks good on TV," Jake commented.

"I don't care," Vicky replied. "It's all because of him that we're the number one story on the news. Now what am I going to do?"

"Nothing," he replied. "It will all blow over. It's just a one day wonder."

But when Jake returned home, later that night, his telephone answering machine light was furiously blinking. When he checked his cell phone that he'd turned off, there were several more messages.

He pressed the play button on the answering machine to hear the chief's voice. "I want you in my office, 8:00 a.m. Monday morning," he ordered. "I think you know why."

CHAPTER NINE

IN THE LAST TWENTY-FOUR hours, the situation in Cobbs Creek had gone from bad to worse. Because of the growing news coverage, there was no greeting from the chief, as he ordered Jake to sit across from him at 8:00 a.m. on Monday morning.

Immediately, Skipper sat, too.

"That's the dog in question?" the chief asked, leaning over his desk.

"Yes, sir. I thought you'd better meet him."

The chief continued to stare at Skipper, who, totally unfazed, stared back. "Smart, is he?"

"Very," Jake replied. "He led me to where Bubba Smith was probably murdered and then he found the body for us."

The chief finally sat back. "And how do you explain all this escalating publicity?"

The previous day, three more TV station vehicles had cruised Cobbs Creek, the several reporters interviewing any resident who would talk to them. Consequently, they were in town for the entire day. That night, the story was not only continued on WQRXTV by Jenny Beale, but also on three more TV stations. To avoid the reporters, Vicky became a virtual prisoner at the cottage, even refusing to answer the telephone. But two of the TV stations managed to get video footage of Jake's arrival, and then in the distance, brief glimpses of the Corgis in the garden.

"We're on TV!" Tango said excitedly that night. "We look really good, don't we?"

"The story was leaked by Mayhew," Jake now replied. "There was nothing I could do to stop him, even if I'd known. Freedom of the press."

The chief grunted. "But this has effectively put the sheriff's department under a microscope. Let's hope these darn reporters never find out who you are and why you're there. I gave you the position so that you'd get to lead the quiet life you wanted."

That thought had been foremost in Jake's mind. "I hope so too, sir. Miss Cooper chose Cobbs Creek for that very reason."

The chief stood, again looking at Skipper. "And as for him, that's not even close to being a police dog. Involving a high profile civilian isn't smart, either. Give him back, get rid of all the reporters, and find another way."

Jake cleared his throat. "With all due respect, sir. I think we need him."

"Why's that exactly?"

Jake looked down at Skipper. "Did you see what happened?"

Skipper barked once.

"Can you help me catch them?"

Skipper barked again.

"So, he can do party tricks," the chief continued. "That's no excuse."

"He can do a lot more than that, sir."

The chief was beginning to realize that Jake wasn't about to back down. "Okay, it is your investigation. It seems that you're still using your unorthodox methods. Keep the dog, if you must. I just don't want to hear about it on the news. Understand?"

"Yes, sir. Perfectly. Thank you."

The chief grunted. "Ask for extra help if you need it. And don't make me a laughing stock for agreeing to this."

"No, sir. We won't," Jake said, as he and Skipper made a fast exit.

Back in the SUV, Jake clipped the deputy's badge on Skipper's collar.

"Now you're official again," Jake said. "But I still think it was a smart idea that you weren't wearing it to meet the chief."

Skipper's reply was to lick Jake's hand.

Tornados are never good news, but later that day, during a bad storm, one touched down in a town less than thirty miles from Cobbs Creek. All that happened in the small community was high winds and torrential rain, but news of the tornado, and the destruction it caused, became the top story on all the networks for the next several days. With news crews rushing to the scene, so that reporters could keep the public continually updated, it diverted their attention away from Jake and Skipper. Much to Jake's relief, the story about them finally became yesterday's news, allowing Jake to finally get back to serious police work.

CHAPTER TEN

IT WASN'T UNTIL VICKY was absolutely sure that the reporters were all gone that she permitted the dogs to go into the garden without her. By now, Skipper was in a routine, waiting by the door every morning to be picked up by Jake, and then running directly to his SUV.

Duke, Misty and Tango were slowly getting used to him not being around during the day, but it didn't mean that they'd given up on the idea of going back to the barn.

For several days, after the story about Skipper and Jake ceased to be of interest, they had been prevented from going outside for very long, due to the bad weather. But finally, the rain stopped and the sun came out.

"We'll go today," Tango whispered at breakfast.

"Only if Mom lets us stay outside," Misty whispered back.

With warm, sunny weather returning, Vicky was happy to see the dogs playing in the garden again.

They waited until they were sure she was at her computer, before squeezing through their hidden escape route and trotting through the marsh to the barn.

Tango reached the hole first. "It's still too small for Duke to get through," she said.

"Maybe Duke can make it bigger?" Misty replied.

"How?"

"He's got big sharp teeth."

"Not as big as his," Duke muttered, making Misty and Tango stop and turn.

Twenty feet away, a huge black and tan dog, with the biggest head they'd ever seen was staring back at them. The hackles on his normally smooth fur were raised, and he had long strands of drool dripping from both sides of his enormous mouth. His menacing growl was unmistakable, and his whole demeanor was not helped by a thick, silver-studded, black leather collar.

He could eat Tango in one bite, Duke was thinking. "Let me handle this," he told them, before anyone could react.

Corgis are used to dealing with animals as big as cows, but not a monster dog with an equally monster mouth and teeth.

As Duke trotted forward, showing no sign of fear, Tango unsuccessfully tried to hide behind Misty, who was already wondering how fast the huge beast could run.

They could all see the dog's muscles rippling under his fur, as Duke reached him, and touched noses.

"Hello, I'm Duke," he said. "Who are you?"

"The man who owns the farm calls me Dog," he replied. "How original is that? It's nice to meet you, too."

"Come and meet my sister Misty, and our niece Tango," Duke continued. "How long have you been here?"

"A few days," Dog replied. "I'm supposed to be the guard dog. Hello," he added, reaching Misty and Tango. "It's nice to have some company."

Tango swallowed. "Hello, Dog," she said.

He gave her a big grin, showing off his a full set of equally big teeth. "Hello, Tango. You're really cute."

Tango blinked. "Thank you."

"Even humans tell her that," Misty said.

"They're not all stupid," Dog replied. "What are you doing?"

"Trying to get into the barn," Duke replied. "Perhaps you could help? Your teeth are bigger than mine."

"I'd be happy to help," Dog replied, stepping forward. "What's in the barn?"

"We need to find out. Do you know?"

Dog shook his head, sending drool in an arc, barely missing Misty.

"Sorry," he continued. "I don't know. The man who now owns me, keeps me chained up most of the time."

"So why not now?" Duke asked.

"Because he's not here," Dog replied.

"Perfect," Misty said. "Can you pull off that piece of wood, for us?"

"No problem."

"Stop," Duke ordered, before Dog could step forward. "Think about it. If we make this hole bigger, Huggins will notice. We need to find a place that he can't see."

"That's easy," Dog said. "Follow me."

Trotting down the length of the barn, Dog quickly disappeared around the far corner.

"He's got no tail like us," Tango remarked, beginning to follow. "What kind of dog is he?"

"I think humans call them Rottweilers," Duke said.

"How does he know that" Tango added to Misty.

"Because he's a lot older than us, that's why."

"That's not the only reason," Duke added.

They found Dog, at another hole in the side wall of the barn, scratching the ground with enormous paws.

"Here would be a good place," he said. "The ground is soft from all the rain, and it's hidden by all these weeds." He took two more steps. "There's also a big bee's nest down there. That's enough to keep most humans away."

"Will they bite us?" Tango asked.

"Not if we don't bother them," Dog replied.

Duke saw no reason to disagree. "But Huggins could still see a hole big enough to get us through."

"Not if Dog could move those," Tango continued, turning to a jumbled pile of rusty, fifty-five gallon drums, mostly hidden by undergrowth.

"Cute, as well as smart," Dog said, with another big grin.

Misty immediately ducked to avoid any possible drool.

"I'll get right on it," Dog added, already beginning to grab the first drum in his enormous mouth.

Tango took several steps backward, in case the drum began to roll. It could, she thought, easily squash her.

As big and strong as he was, even Dog was having trouble moving the drum.

"Let me help," Duke said, pulling from the other end.

"Me too," Misty added, trying to get a grip on the rusty metal.

"Why not roll it?" Tango asked. "Then none of you will get hurt."

"Why didn't I think of that," Dog replied, now putting both front paws on the drum, and pushing hard. "Look out."

Duke and Misty just got out of the way in time, as the drum broke free of the weeds and rolled quickly, coming to a stop with a loud thump against the barn's wood planking.

No one moved.

Dog slowly looked around. "I don't think anyone heard us."

"Just as well," Duke said. "You live here. We don't. I think you're here to stop us. Your owner isn't a nice man."

"I know he isn't," Dog replied. "How was I supposed to stop you?"

Duke had a very good imagination. "I'd rather not say. But I like you much more as a friend, rather than the enemy."

Dog caught on quickly. "I just look ferocious."

"But the humans don't know that. And your breed can be trained."

"Point taken. But you're quite safe with me."

"Phew. That's a relief," Misty muttered.

"Don't we have a barn to get into?" Tango interrupted. "Huggins might come back soon."

Using his large teeth to full advantage, Dog easily removed a small part of the lowest plank, and along with Tango's digging skills, they soon had a hole large enough for all three Corgis to squeeze through.

"If we make it any bigger, we run the risk of Huggins seeing," Duke said to Dog.

"No problem," Dog replied. "I'll stay out here and keep watch. After all," he added with big grin, "it's what I'm supposed to do."

Duke then squeezed through the hole to find Misty and Tango sniffing around a stack of cardboard boxes in the gloomy interior.

"Can you smell it?" Tango asked.

Duke ran his nose down the side of the nearest box. "Yes. But I don't know what it is."

"We can tear off the cardboard," Misty said. "See what's inside."

"Not a good idea," Duke replied. "The humans will notice."

"So how do we find out?"

"Dog can be our eyes and ears," Duke continued. "He can keep watch and tell us what happens. It's safer that way."

Back outside, they found Dog scratching at the weeds. "Hiding the trail," he explained.

Tango studied the pile of drums again. "If you moved the one with the big hole, we could leave it at the side of the barn, and then squeeze through both holes."

"Your niece is very smart," Dog said to Duke. "She must take after you."

With a lot more pushing, the drum lay on its side, against the hole, while another stood blocking one of the two open ends. The dogs finally stood back to admire their work, panting hard.

"It looks really good," Dog said. "But I need a drink."

Misty agreed. "Me too."

"I think we all do," Duke added.

"There's big bowl of water in the yard," Dog continued. "Help yourselves."

"My half-brother Skipper is working with the local sheriff," Duke told Dog. "If you see another Corgi, he's one of us. I thought you should know. Huggins has already threatened him, so he hates him, too."

"That's good to know," Dog replied. "Thanks."

Then following Dog's brisk trot, they were about to turn into the courtyard, when they all heard the now familiar sound of the pickup.

"Not again," Duke said.

"Go," Dog ordered. "I'll keep him busy. Come back soon."

Careful not to be seen, the Corgis slunk back through the marsh, while Dog gave Huggins such a long, enthusiastic greeting that this time the dogs were able to escape unseen.

"I thought you said the dog was vicious?" the man with Huggins said, getting slowly out of the pickup and keeping his distance.

"He is," Huggins replied. "But not with me. Want me to show you?"

"No, thanks," the man continued. He eyed the large Rottweiler. "I believe you."

Some humans are so stupid, Dog thought, sitting at the side of the pickup as the men disappeared into the house.

A few minutes later, they reappeared, heading toward the barn.

"Come, Dog," Huggins called out, and reaching the barn doors, he unlocked a shiny new padlock attached to a heavy chain.

"So where's the merchandise?" Huggins' visitor asked, looking around.

Huggins laughed. "In here."

The man looked again. "I can't see it. You're fooling me, Ralph?"

"No," Huggins said. "But that's the point, Phil. If that nosy sheriff comes around again, for whatever reason, he won't find it either."

Sitting quietly by the doors, Dog was taking it all in, especially when Huggins reached through the wall of rotting hay bales, and unlocked a very well camouflaged door.

"Well, look at that," Phil exclaimed, studying the door, with several hay bales attached to the outside. "No one will ever find that."

Unless I show them, Dog thought, and moved silently closer.

At the door, he peered carefully inside to see Huggins and the man called Phil opening one of the many cardboard boxes.

"Toilet paper?" Phil asked, holding up a small clear package, filled with a white powder.

"Not only toilet rolls, but paper towel, household cleaner, and of course, baking flour. Everything the poor and needy can use," Huggins replied.

"You're a real saint."

Huggins laughed. "Well, I'm not your average drug dealer. That's a fact. But a saint? Never."

"So how do we move it?" Phil continued.

"Chuck Gaston's bringing the boat up here in the next few days. He'll tell me when. We need a late night, high tide. Then we load the boat with what I've already packaged, and off it goes."

"Nice little operation," Phil commented as the door closed. "Quiet and out of the way. It was a good plan."

"I think so," Huggins replied, locking the barn door again. "And it's even safer now that Dog is here."

I wouldn't count on it, Dog thought, following Huggins back across the courtyard.

"That was way too close again," Duke remarked, as they all squeezed under the fence and back into the garden. "We have to come up with a better idea."

"We'll ask Skipper tonight," Tango said.

"Why do you think he has the answer to everything?"

"I bet he'd have know Dog was a Rottweiler, too," she replied.

"Tango's got a point," Misty said. "He's the one spending all day with Jake. That's who we really need."

"Now, I agree," Duke said.

"Jake keeps talking about proof," Skipper told them, later that night.

"What's that?" Tango asked.

"It means that we need to get into those boxes and find out what's inside," Duke said, before Skipper could answer.

"Dog said he'd help us," Misty added.

"I don't know how," Duke replied. "But let's hope he finds a way."

CHAPTER ELEVEN

THE FOLLOWING MORNING, JAKE stopped the SUV in the courtyard of Huggins' farmhouse, but on seeing the huge Rottweiler, even though it was attached to a long heavy chain, he decided to leave Skipper in the truck.

On hearing Dog's loud, angry barking, Huggins soon appeared.

"Morning, Sheriff," Huggins said, approaching the SUV, as Jake got out. "Meet Dog. What do you think of him?"

"He's big. Got a license, Ralph?"

Huggins laughed. "Of course. I'm not in the habit of breaking the law. Want to check? I've got the paperwork inside."

"I wouldn't have thought you needed a guard dog?" Jake added, following him into the house.

"My cousin was murdered. You can't be too careful," Huggins replied.

At the kitchen table, Jake told him the reason he was there, and then showed Huggins several photographs of known criminals from a file folder.

Huggins appeared to slowly study the images, but then said that he didn't know the men, and had certainly never seen them.

Not fully convinced, Jake finally closed the folder, and thanked him for his time.

"Sorry, I was no help," Huggins said. "But I'm glad you're not giving up."

"It's not my style," Jake replied

In the courtyard, Jake had misjudged the length of Dog's chain. From his seat in the SUV, Skipper watched as the huge dog came toward him. Instinct told him to growl and bark a warning, but before he had the chance, Dog put his paws on the side of the truck, his big wet nose pressed against the passenger door window.

"You must be Dog," Skipper said through the cracked window. "I'm Duke and Misty's half-brother."

"It's good to meet you," Dog replied. "If the humans see us, let's give them a show?"

Skipper grinned. "Good idea. They told me you were smart."

"Not as smart as little Tango. She's so cute. What's the sheriff doing here?"

"He's got pictures of some bad men to show to Huggins, in case if he recognizes any of them."

"Do you?" Dog asked.

"From what little I saw? No."

"There was a another man here yesterday," Dog continued. "Huggins called him Phil and showed him how to get into the barn. There's a hidden door..."

But before Dog could continue, Jake reappeared.

"Show time!" Dog barked.

"Go for it!" Skipper barked back.

All Jake and Huggins saw was two dogs attempting to kill each other, and only the window of the SUV was stopping them.

"I'll pay for your damaged paintwork," Huggins shouted above the noise, using all his strength to pull Dog away. "Sorry, Sheriff. I had no idea he'd try to kill your dog. Mind you," Huggins added, breathing hard as he finally got Dog under control. "He's a feisty little thing."

Jake quickly eyed the damage. "I'll bring you the bill, next time I'm over."

"No problem. But call first. I'll make sure Dog's locked up."

That's not good, Skipper was thinking, as Jake climbed behind the wheel. Then he leaned across to stroke Skipper's raised fur.

"Easy, Buddy," Jake said. "That's one dog you really don't want to mess with."

But as Jake drove away, he couldn't help thinking that Skipper didn't seem that rattled at the encounter as he settled happily on the seat. *Was it an act? No, that's not possible, is it?*

"Any luck?" Hank asked, when Jake entered the office.

"According to Huggins? No."

"But you don't believe him?"

"As much as I believe he'll pay for the damage on the SUV." Then Jake went on to explain.

"So Huggins got a big guard dog?" Hank asked after Jake had finished. "What's he got to guard? A lot of junk and scrap metal."

"Exactly," Jake replied. "He says it's because of what happened to Bubba, but I think that's just a weak excuse. And explain to me why he's now got a new chain and padlock on the old barn?"

"I can't," Hank began, as the telephone rang and he answered the call. "Mrs. Foster's locked herself out again," he added, after hanging up.

"I'll go. You went the last time," Jake said, getting to his feet. "Skipper stay," he continued. "It's too hot for you to be sitting in the truck."

Skipper watched Jake leave, before laying down by his chair.

Hank answered two more phone calls, before he too got up. "I'm going to get lunch," he said to Skipper. "You stay here. I'll be back soon"

Skipper saw the office door close, and as soon as he heard Hank lock it, he jumped onto Jake's chair. Then it was just an easy leap to

Jake's desktop, and the file folder with the photographs of the men that Huggins denied knowing. Of course, he couldn't read, but he could recognize some images. He pawed through six pages, two of them floating to the floor, but none of the men looked familiar to him.

Jake and Hank returned to the office together, sandwiches in hand, along with Skipper's roast beef and cheese roll.

"What's this mess?" Jake immediately asked Hank. "Never leave my desk like this again."

"I haven't been near your desk," Hank replied. "Honest."

"Well, someone has."

"I don't know who," Hank interrupted. "I locked the door, like you said, before going to get lunch."

"You didn't go through the folder?"

"Why should I? I put it together for you. It wasn't as if I didn't know what was in it."

The men stared silently at each other, before turning slowly to Skipper.

"The dog did this?" Hank continued. "No way."

"Got a better explanation?" Jake asked.

"No, but how? And why? And don't tell me he can read?"

Jake chuckled. "I know he can't read. And he can't clean up after himself either. But I suspect he might be able to recognize faces."

Hank began to laugh. "That's one real special dog. And no, you can't have my job," he added to Skipper.

Skipper tried to ignore them. *That was stupid,* he thought, before Jake gave him the roast beef and cheese. *I'll have to be more careful.*

It was well after midnight as Dog lay at the side of the barn, his heavy chain stretched to its full length. But he wasn't asleep. From his position, and by the light of a full moon, he could see through the rusty wire fence and across the marsh to the area of trees and undergrowth.

Somewhere behind those trees is where the Corgis live, he thought. *They're really nice, and they're right about Huggins. He's a very bad man. He wants me to attack and kill Skipper, but it's not in my nature to do such a terrible thing. Any human who would leave me outside, when I'm used to a caring owner and a nice warm bed, will never get me to agree to do anything like that. I'd much rather bite Huggins. Maybe, I'll get my chance soon. And I bet if I bark loud enough during the day, the Corgis will hear me and come back. Until then, I've got to do some exploring on my own.*

Dog eventually closed his eyes and drifted off into a very uneasy sleep, all the time being watched by a large grey owl on the roof of the barn.

CHAPTER TWELVE

DOG HAD SEARCHED HIS doggy brain with ways to get the attention of his new Corgi friends. He was usually kept on a chain when Huggins was around, and as Dog couldn't see beyond the barrier of trees and undergrowth at the far side of the marsh, where he knew they lived, he concluded that the simplest method was the best. He barked. Loudly. He also realized that this was a very hit and miss method. Not only did he and his new friends have to be free of humans, but they had to also hear him and escape. It was a long way across the marsh to the cottage, so even his nose couldn't tell him when the Corgis were outside. But when the wind was in the right direction, even Vicky heard him.

"That's the third time this week, I've heard a dog bark," she said in the garden, several days later. "Ralph Huggins must have bought one. What do you think, guys?" She looked down. "He doesn't sound too happy."

He's not, and he's calling us, Skipper thought, looking back.

"I'm going in," Vicky continued. "Go play, and behave yourselves."

Highly unlikely, Duke was thinking.

"She's gone," Tango said, watching Vicky disappear into the cottage. "Can we go now? Dog wants us."

"I know," Skipper replied. "Patience."

"You don't have any."

"Not with you, I don't," he snapped. "Do you want us to get caught?"

Tango didn't reply, but slunk quickly away to be with Misty. "What are you doing?"

"Looking for lizards," Misty replied. "They're easier to find and chase than squirrels. You can sneak up on them. Quick, there's one!"

"She'll learn," Duke said to Skipper, glancing in Tango's direction. "She's still very young."

"And exceptionally smart. That's why she needs to learn now." Skipper watched as Misty and Tango seemed to be successfully herding lizards into a bush. "Let's go," he added. "While they're occupied."

Duke gave a final backward glance at his sister and niece, before following Skipper down the lawn, and through the bushes to their escape route.

In the distance, they heard Dog bark again. "I'm alone. Come now, if you can."

"We're on our way," Skipper barked back.

Then he and Duke squeezed under the fence and began trotting toward the farm.

By the time they were half way across the marsh, Misty and Tango had caught up with them.

"You were going without us?" Tango asked.

Skipper stopped and faced her. "No. But you have to learn to listen to me. Otherwise, you could get hurt, or worse. Is that understood?"

With her ears back, she bowed her head in submission. "I understand."

"Good," he replied. "Then let's find Dog."

Dog had already seen the Corgis coming through the marsh, and was waiting for them by the barb wire fence. Skipper was through first, followed by Duke, Misty and finally Tango.

"Good to see you all," Dog barked. "I was beginning to think that you would never get out."

"Us too," Tango whispered.

"I wasn't expecting you," Dog said to Skipper. "Why aren't you with Jake?"

"I stay home on his days off," Skipper replied. "That's why I'm here."

"Good deal," Dog continued. "Huggins has gone, so we're quite safe."

"Unless any other humans show up," Duke muttered.

"Apart from that man Phil, no other human has been here," Dog added. "Time to check out those boxes?"

"I'm ready," Tango said. Then she stopped. "I'll follow you."

With Skipper and Dog in the lead, they headed around the far corner of the barn to their secret hole and the fifty-five gallon drums.

"No one has found it," Dog said. "I made sure of that."

"Thanks," Skipper replied, squeezing through the drum and hole.

"I'm too big to get through," Dog said when all four Corgis were inside the darken room. "What do you see?"

"There's a lot more boxes," Tango replied.

"Huggins brought them in the pickup, with that man Phil, last night," Dog continued. "It was very late. That's why he's not here today. He said he had to go back to Florida. Isn't that a long way?"

"Lucky for us, yes," Duke answered, from somewhere in the dark. "What is that smell?"

"I don't know," Skipper said. "But it's not nice. I think it's very dangerous."

"Dangerous how?" Tango asked.

He faced her. "I don't know. But you mustn't touch it. Do you understand?"

"Yes," she replied.

"We need to get a box open," Skipper added. "You have sharp little teeth. You try first."

Tango stepped forward, and began chewing on a side seam of the closest box. When the cardboard got soggy enough, she pawed at it with small feet and claws, until she'd made a small hole.

"My turn," Skipper told her. "Step back."

He managed to grab enough of the cardboard to pull, and as he clamped down harder with his teeth and began to tug hard, the cardboard finally ripped. Several little plastic bags spilled onto the dirt floor.

For a moment, the dogs could only stare, then Duke took a step forward and very carefully sniffed. "I don't know what it is. But I do know it's something we shouldn't touch."

"I agree," Skipper said.

"So how are we going to tell Jake?" Tango asked.

"Misty is going to carry one back home," Skipper replied.

Misty faced her brother. "I am? Why me?"

"Because," Skipper continued. "You're a girl, and used to carrying puppies. You'll be more careful than…"

"I'm a girl," Tango interrupted.

"You're still too young."

"I don't have puppies," Misty said.

"But you've got all the right instincts," Skipper replied.

Until Tango arrived in the household, both humans and dogs noticed that Misty retained all her puppy qualities. Even Vicky began to wonder if Misty was ever going to grow up. But with a new baby niece in their midst, Misty's maternal instincts took over. From day one, she became very motherly and protective, and now that Tango was older, they were still best friends.

"Okay, I'll do it," Misty said, before gently picking up one corner of the bag.

"Don't bite down," Skipper ordered, as they made their way back into the sunlight.

Dog immediately sniffed the small package, and took two steps back.

"That could really hurt us," he stated. "Be very careful."

"We will," Skipper replied. "Sorry we can't stay, this time. We've got to get home."

"I understand," Dog continued. "Please come back soon?"

"We'll try," Duke said, as they wiggled under the lowest strand of barb wire. "That's a promise."

The Corgis route back to the garden was taken slowly and with great care.

At the cottage, Skipper told Misty to go through the pet door, and drop the small plastic baggy on the kitchen tile, where Vicky would see it. Then she was to come back outside, as though nothing had happened.

Misty's mission was successfully completed, and just in time. Less than five minutes after dropping the package, Vicky entered the kitchen to refill her coffee mug.

What's this? she thought, bending down to take a closer look.

Then she picked up the small baggy and discovered that the top was still wet with saliva. She held it up to the light, studying the contents, before looking through the window to see if the dogs were in view. When she couldn't see them, she left the baggy on the counter and went outside to check.

She soon found Misty and Tango were busy rounding up lizards, Duke was exploring the hibiscus bushes, a favorite spot, and Skipper was slowly following the pungent smell of a wild mink. Although mink are common in coastal Georgia, they're rarely seen by humans, who often mistake them for escaped ferrets. While ferrets have a dull coat, mink are still prized for their distinctive and glossy fur, although all Skipper knew was that they smelled really interesting.

Nothing unusual, Vicky was thinking as she looked around. *But how did that baggy get inside? It had to be them.*

Back in the kitchen, and after looking closely again at the baggy, Vicky picked up the telephone.

"If you're not too busy, there's something here I think you should see," she told Jake.

He arrived, fifteen minutes later, dressed in a tee shirt and shorts.

That was quick, Duke barked, as he and his siblings rushed through the pet door to greet him.

"Sorry to get you out here on your day off," Vicky said. "But I wouldn't have done it if I didn't think it was important."

Jake smiled. "Anytime. You know that. So where's the fire?" He then bent down to stroke all four Corgis.

Vicky held up the baggy.

Jake took it, and studied it carefully, without comment. "Where did you get this?" he eventually asked.

Vicky told him. "...And it was still wet with saliva. The dogs had to have found it," she ended.

"Do you know what it is?" he asked.

"If I had to make an educated guess, I'd say it looks like drugs."

"I think you're right, and I'll know for sure, after the contents are tested. But I'm almost sure it's heroin. Really bad stuff." He turned to face four pairs of dark eyes. "Which one of you found this? And where?"

"It's at times like this, I really wish they could talk," Vicky commented.

Us too, the dogs thought in unison.

"Listen to me," Jake added, waving the baggy. "This is bad. Really bad. You mustn't touch. Understand?"

We know that, Skipper thought, and gave a short bark.

"I think they get it," Vicky said.

"I agree," Jake replied. "Sorry, but I've got to go. This's something that can't wait."

"I know," she continued. "See you for dinner tonight?"

"Count on it."

As Jake's SUV left the driveway, Vicky faced the dogs. "You are not to do anything like that again. The powder in that baggy could kill you. Do I make myself clear?"

Skipper gave a short bark.

"Mom's mad with us," Tango whispered.

"Only because it's really dangerous and she doesn't wants us to get hurt," Duke whispered back.

"I did warn you," Skipper said.

"We know," Misty replied.

"You took a huge risk," Skipper continued to Misty. "But we've done what needed to be done."

"Does that mean we can't see Dog again?" Tango interrupted.

"Not at all," Skipper added. "But no more going into the barn. That's an order."

"We got it the first time," Duke muttered.

Chapter Thirteen

It had been several days since Jake had taken the baggy. In a his recent telephone call to Vicky, he'd told her that the crime lab confirmed the contents of the baggy was indeed heroin, and packaged to be sold on the streets to both adults and kids. In fact, anyone who could pay. As Vicky replaced the receiver, an idea began to form.

Time to say hello to my new neighbor, she thought, opening a large kitchen cabinet. *Let's hope I've got some Brownie mix.*

Even in small quantities chocolate can kill dogs, but that didn't stop the Corgis from wanting it. Just the smell of the Brownies cooking, brought them in from outside. Lizards were forgotten, and Duke's exploring was temporarily halted, as a delicious aroma wafted across the garden.

By the time Vicky removed the Brownies from the oven, she had the dog's full attention.

"You're just waiting for me to drop them," she said, laughing. "Sorry, guys, you're out of luck."

"Just a small piece?" Tango barked.

"And for me," Misty added.

"It's supposed to be bad for us," Duke said.

"How can something that tastes so good be bad?" Tango asked.

"I don't know," he replied. "But it is."

But their patience was rewarded.

"As it's mostly cake mix, you can have a small piece," Vicky told them, after cutting the Brownies into squares and placing them in a plastic container. "But don't tell Skipper."

No way, Misty thought.

"I'll be back soon," she continued. "I'm off to see Mr. Huggins." Then picking up the container, she left the cottage, locking the door behind her.

The Corgis heard the garage door open and close, and the sound of her SUV begin to fade.

"She's gone," Duke said.

"She's giving Brownies to that nasty man? Why?" Tango asked.

"It's what humans do," he replied.

"What a waste of really good food," Misty muttered, leaving the kitchen through the pet door.

It occurred to Vicky, as she drove down the rutted and still weedy track to the farm that she should have maybe called Ralph Huggins, before driving over.

If he's not home, I'll just leave the Brownies by the door with a note, she thought, entering the courtyard.

But to her rising apprehension, Huggins' pickup was standing by the old barn doors.

Vicky parked next to it, and as she got out, she could hear the deep bark of a large dog. Seconds later, Huggins came out of the barn.

She noticed that he almost squeezed through the doors, before padlocking them.

Vicky smiled, and held up the container. "I'm your neighbor Vicky Cooper. I'm sorry I haven't been over sooner, but I thought you'd like these to welcome you to Cobbs Creek."

Huggins approached slowly, and took the container. "Brownies?" he said looking inside. "That's mighty kind of you, ma'am."

"It's Vicky, please."

"Well then, Vicky, let me return your Southern hospitality. A drink maybe?"

"Thank you. That would be very nice."

All Huggins knew about his closest neighbor was that she wrote best selling murder mysteries, and that she owned four pesky little varmints that he like to see gone. Permanently. What he didn't know, and was about to discover, was that Vicky was also very good at extracting information.

"I assume you must have a dog?" she asked, as she followed Huggins into the kitchen. "I sometimes hear it bark. It is yours?"

Huggins nodded. "Beer okay?"

"No thanks, I'm driving. Hot tea if you have it. So where's your dog?"

"Locked up," Huggins replied. "Nasty brute. Wouldn't want him getting out and hurting someone. Tea it is."

To Huggins, the Brownies tasted really good, as he ate his third, while Vicky sipped a mug of micro-waved tea.

As time ticked by, he begrudgingly had to admit that having an attractive young woman at his kitchen table made a very pleasant change. But little did he realize, as the friendly and seemingly harmless conversation progressed that he was being pumped for information.

"...so you have big plans for the farm?" Vicky asked. "I'd love to see the house. I've got remodeling in my blood, so I'm told."

"If you don't mind the mess and the dirt?"

"Not at all," she replied, leaving the tea. "Lead the way."

They eventually began to climb the stairs to the second floor, when Huggins stopped.

"Did you know my cousin Bubba?" he asked.

"I met him once," she replied truthfully. "After what happened, I wish I'd taken the time to get to know him better."

Huggins grunted. "Never know what life's going to throw at you."

How true, she thought, continuing the climb, as Huggins checked his watch for the third time in as many minutes. "I'm keeping you? I'm sorry."

"Don't be," he replied. "We'd better get back downstairs. Up here can be dangerous. The floor's rotting in places where the rain comes in."

Back in the courtyard, Huggins relief that she was finally leaving was short lived.

"I didn't realize there was a milking shed," Vicky remarked, already heading toward it, forcing Huggins to follow. "How great it would be to have cows in here again." She disappeared inside, before he could stop her.

As far as Huggins was concerned, Vicky seemed to know a lot about cows, which was of no interest to him as she continued to talk, all the while scanning the shed for anything that seemed out of place.

"I also love old barns," she continued, beginning to leave the milking shed, and catching Huggins by surprise. "There can be so much history in them."

But before Huggins could stop her, he was saved by Jake.

As Vicky reached the barn doors, Jake's SUV swung into the courtyard.

"Miss Cooper?" Jake said as he got out. "This's a surprise."

She could tell from his expression that he wasn't at all pleased to see her there, while Skipper jumped up and down on the seat, barking in excitement at seeing her.

"I was just leaving," she replied. "Enjoy the rest of the Brownies, Ralph."

"Will do. Thanks." He turned to Jake: "Seems to be my day for visitors."

"Want to take Skipper home?" Jake called out, making Vicky stop. "We've almost finished our rounds."

"Good idea," she said.

But as Jake opened the door to the SUV, expecting Skipper to go straight to her, instead, he ran to the barn doors

"What's going on?" he barked at Dog on the other side.

"I'm locked in," Dog barked back.

"Need help?"

Dog began pawing furiously at the bottom of the doors. "Get me out!"

"You'd better call your dog off," Huggins shouted above the noise. "My dog will kill yours, if you don't."

By now, Vicky had snatched the leash from Jake's hand, and was at Skipper's side. She couldn't see Huggins' dog, but she knew from the sound it was making, that Skipper wouldn't stand a chance.

Leashed and at her heels, Vicky quickly led him away.

"And keep him off my property," Huggins added. "That's if you know what's good for you."

Vicky spun to face him. "It was an accident. There's no need to be so nasty."

"I hope you choke on the Brownies," she muttered, putting her SUV into gear, and glaring at Huggins through the windshield as she drove away.

"Apart from making threats to a neighbor, I'll also cite you for keeping a dangerous dog," Jake said.

Huggins forced a smile. "Said in the heat of the moment, Sheriff."

"I hope so, Ralph. I strongly suggest that you apologize. Do I make myself clear?"

"Sure do. What did you want?"

"It can wait," Jake replied. "Some other day. And remember what I said."

Huggins was still swearing under his breath as Jake also drove away.

Later that night, over dinner at the cottage, Vicky got quite a lecture from Jake.

"…so stay away from Huggins and the farm," Jake ended. "You're playing with fire, and I don't want to see you or the Corgis get hurt. Promise me."

"I promise," Vicky quietly replied.

CHAPTER FOURTEEN

THE VEHEMENCE OF JAKE's dinnertime lecture had shocked Vicky. She was beginning to understand how Tango felt after being chastised by Skipper. In the months that she'd known Jake, she'd never asked about his background, and he hadn't offered to tell her. But she now knew that he wasn't your typical small town sheriff.

Two days later, with Skipper away with Jake, she at first ignored Duke, Misty and Tango's barking. When they didn't stop, she began to leave her office. As she did, the doorbell rang. When she peered through the glass and saw Ralph Huggins, she almost didn't open the door. But he saw her and gave a small wave.

"I'll be right with you," she shouted through the door, and with Skipper not being around, it was relatively easy, as Duke was so well behaved, to get the dogs into her office and shut them in.

Then she opened the front door.

"Is this a bad time?" Huggins asked.

Vicky shrugged. "I was writing."

"Yeah, I was told you're a writer. Mysteries, isn't it?"

"That's right. Is there something you wanted?"

Huggins shuffled his feet. "Can I come in? I won't keep you long."

"Of course. Follow me."

Vicky noticed that Huggins was taking a good look around as he entered the kitchen. "Nice place you've got here."

"Thanks," she replied. "It had a lot of potential."

"You did good. Is that why you're interested in the farm?"

She smiled. *He's on a fishing expedition.* "Absolutely. Older houses are much more interesting, even when they're updated, don't you think?"

Whether he did or didn't Huggins wasn't about to say.

"You need help remodeling?" Vicky continued. "That's why you're here?"

"No," he said quickly. "I came to say I may have been a bit harsh with you the other day. No hard feelings?"

"If that's an apology, I accept," she said. "Coffee?"

"Sure, why not, I got time."

You ungracious thug, she was thinking as she made a fresh pot. "I hope you don't mind, but I have to let the dogs out."

Without waiting for his reply, she disappeared down the hallway.

No sooner had Vicky opened her office door, than the dogs shot passed her. They loved company and usually gave everyone a loud and enthusiastic greeting. But as she followed them, she saw them skid to a halt, and their barking immediately stopped.

Huggins had made himself at home, by sitting on a bar height chair at the raised counter, and was now surround by three angry Corgis.

"Not very friendly, are they," Huggins commented.

Vicky stopped herself from saying, they usually are. "Maybe they can smell your dog," she said instead.

But as Huggins drained his coffee and got ready to leave, there was no mistaking the low ominous growl, times three.

"Let me take the dogs outside," she continued. "I wouldn't want you to lose a leg."

Huggins couldn't tell if she was being serious or not, but stayed seated, just in case.

With the dogs safely in the garden, and the pet door closed, Vicky returned to the kitchen.

"I gotta go," Huggins said, already on his feet. "That was good coffee."

"I'm glad you liked it," she replied. "Stop by anytime."

But she noted, Huggins almost ran to his pickup, and drove away with a squeal of tires.

Good riddance, she thought, watching him leave.

That evening, during dinner, when she casually mention to Jake that Huggins had been to see her, he exploded.

"I do not want you or the Corgis going anywhere near him, or the farm. Is that clearly understood?" he snapped. "Are you looking for trouble?"

"He came to see me," she replied. "To apologize."

"So you think. Men like Huggins don't do that without good reason. Trust me, he wasn't just being neighborly."

"Duke, Misty and Tango didn't think so either," she continued quietly.

"Then trust their instincts. I mean that."

"Jake sounds mad," Tango whispered from under the table.

"He is," Duke said.

"So how do we get back to the farm?" Misty asked.

"Don't worry, we'll think of a way," Duke replied.

"Skipper will know," Tango continued.

"Not necessarily," Duke added. "Now start looking cute, if you want leftovers."

CHAPTER FIFTEEN

WITH MUCH COOLER DAYTIME temperatures, Vicky decided that on this particular afternoon, to take the dogs for a walk beyond the garden and into Cobbs Creek.

Excited to be away from the cottage, Duke and Misty, on a double leash, were pulling Vicky along, while Tango, who was used to being paired with Skipper, did her best to follow their lead.

"We can take Mom to the farm," Duke said, "if we keep this up."

"Good idea. Keep pulling," Misty replied.

"I'm trying," Tango added.

Duke suddenly swerved toward the marsh. "Now!" he barked.

Vicky was almost dragged off her feet, as all three Corgis aimed for a small path.

"I understand," she said. "The marsh it is, if that's where you want to go. But slow down."

"It's working," Tango barked. "Keep going Uncle Duke."

"I am," he replied.

On finally reaching the rusty barbed wire fence, Vicky stopped. "On Jake's orders, this's as far as we go."

"No it isn't," Duke stated, crawling under the wire, before Vicky could stop him.

With Duke now on the other side, Misty quickly followed. Tango took a different route, leaving Vicky with a tangled mess of leashes.

"Now look what you've done," she said, and realized that the only way to get the leashes untangled was to unclip them

"Stay," she ordered, as she freed Duke.

He waited until all of them were off the leash, before he took off toward the barn, with Misty and Tango in hot pursuit. They quickly disappeared from view, leaving Vicky with no alternative, but to climb the fence and follow.

She kept calling to them, and was very surprised when they didn't obey and come back.

They're in a lot of trouble, she thought, rounding the corner into the courtyard. All she saw was Huggins' red pickup, but still no sign of the dogs. Then she heard Duke give a low bark, and as she turned, she could see him in the open doorway of the barn.

As she stepped in his direction, he backed into the barn and disappeared again.

What odd behavior. I'll get them for this, she thought, approaching the barn door and looking inside.

Duke, Misty and Tango were all now standing against a tall stack of rotting hay bales and they refused to move when Vicky called them again.

She waved the leashes as she stepped toward them. "Come here, right now!"

The dogs barked their warning too late, as the camouflaged door in the stack suddenly opened, catching Vicky by stunned surprise.

"Well, well," Huggins sneered. "It's my nosy neighbor again." He took a step toward her, and before she could run, he quickly grabbed her arm. "Gottcha."

"Let me go!" she shouted, trying to twist free from his vice-like grip. "You'll be sorry if you don't."

Huggins suddenly yelled, as Duke gave him a well aimed bite on his ankle, although Duke narrowly avoided being kicked when Huggins lashed out. But the dogs weren't about to give up as Vicky continued to shout and struggle. Just as Misty and Tango were about to continue Duke's work, to Vicky's increasing horror, Huggins aimed a gun at them.

"Call your dogs off before I shoot them," he ordered, still grimacing with pain. "And believe me, I'd like nothing better than to dispatch the wretched little varmints, right now."

But Duke, Misty and Tango were now so angry, they circled Huggins, ready for a three-pronged attack.

"I'm warning you!" Huggins shouted, tightening his grip on Vicky's arm. "I'll kill them."

"Sit, guys," she commanded. "I'm okay. Just sit. Please."

"Do as she says," Duke whispered as he sat. "We'll think of another way."

Reluctantly, Tango obeyed, but Misty held her ground, teeth still bared.

"You'd better control it," Huggins added, now waving the gun in Misty's direction. "One shot, that's all it's going to take."

"Misty, sit!"

She finally obeyed, glaring at Huggins.

Vicky was then pushed roughly through the door, with the gun barrel now held against her lower back.

"Call your dogs," Huggins ordered. "That's if you ever want to see them again."

"Here, guys," Vicky said.

Slowly, following Duke's lead, they entered the darkened room.

At that moment, Phil appeared, with Dog on a leash.

"Perfect timing," Huggins said. "Tie her up," he added, pointing at Vicky. "Then lock her in. If those dogs try to escape, set Dog on them. In the meantime, I'll hold him."

Phil handed Dog's leash to Huggins.

"What do you want me to do?" Dog barked.

"Go with them," Duke barked back. "Find out where they're going. We'll try and escape, but you know where we are, if we can't."

Dog pretended to lunge at Tango. "Don't worry," he growled. "I'll come back for you."

He then strained on the shortened leash, almost pulling Huggins off his feet. "It's show time!"

Immediately, all the dogs began barking and growling, convincing the humans that they were about to witness a bloody dog fight to the death.

"Hurry!" Huggins shouted to Phil above the noise. "It's time to go."

"I'll see you pay..." But Vicky never finished the sentence, as already tied to a wooden chair by her hands and feet, Phil's last act was to cover her mouth with duct tape.

Then everything was plunged into darkness as the door closed and they heard the click of a lock.

"Look," Huggins said to Phil outside the barn, mistaking Dog's reluctance to leave. "He still wants to kill the little varmints. Maybe, I'll let him. When it gets dark, take him to Chuck. He's needed on the boat. He'll make sure our merchandise gets safely to its destination. In the meantime, I'll clean up here."

"Will do," Phil replied, dragging a still reluctant Dog away.

Duke, Misty and Tango eyes adjusted quickly to the dark, and all they could hear now was Vicky making odd noises.

At first, the dogs hadn't known what to do, so they waited at the door, listening for any sound coming from beyond the room.

When Duke's low growl woke Vicky from a doze, the room was even darker and she guessed that it was several hours later.

"I can hear Dog leaving," Duke whispered. "We have to do something."

Vicky was now stiff and very frightened, and attempted to move, trying again to speak.

"What can we do?" Misty asked.

"Mom's trying to say something," Tango added. "I'll find out what."

To Vicky's surprise, Tango suddenly jumped onto her lap, and licked her face. Although Tango couldn't understand why Vicky couldn't talk, she could taste the salty tears rolling down her cheeks.

"Mom's crying," Tango said.

"Let me see," Misty replied, also jumping onto Vicky's lap, and almost knocking her niece out of the way.

Vicky tried to tell them to pull off the duct tape, but all the dogs heard were strange mumbling sounds.

"What's this?" Misty asked, licking the tape.

"I don't know," Tango replied, licking again.

Vicky nodded her head.

"Mom wants us to stop?" Tango asked.

"No, she wants you to keep licking," Duke said, watching closely.

"It's something sticky," Tango continued.

Vicky tried to nod faster, without making the dogs stop.

"Pull it," Duke said.

"I'm trying."

"Try harder."

To give Tango more space to pull, Misty jumped down, and Vicky put her head back, and turned it slightly as small, very sharp teeth gripped one small corner of the tape and it slowly began to lift.

"Keep pulling!" Misty barked.

Tango was too busy trying to keep her balance on Vicky's lap to reply.

As the tape lifted a little more, Vicky suddenly turned her head sharply away, and with a ripping sound, the duct tape finally came free of her mouth.

She let out a long sigh. "Thank you. Thank you," she said quietly. "You're all so smart."

Tango, still on Vicky's lap, was now trying in a cat-like manner to clean the sticky stuff off her mouth and whiskers, while the remains of the duct tape dangled from the side of Vicky's mouth. But she could finally speak again.

"Now all I have to do is get you to untie me," she said.

Duke attempted to pull on the rope that Phil had used to tie Vicky's ankles to the chair, but the knots seemed to be getting tighter instead of loosening. He then balanced on his hind legs, but the knots around Vicky's wrists were no better.

"We need to get help," Duke said. "If our hole is still there, we can get out that way."

Misty went to check. "They pushed the boxes up against the wall. Even Tango couldn't wiggle through."

"Let me see," Tango said, jumping off Vicky's lap, but she soon discovered that Misty was correct.

"Plan B," Tango added, looking at the wall of boxes.

Before Duke and Misty could stop her, she backed up, and a split second later, she was sprinting across the room. In one gigantic leap, Tango went airborne. Luckily for her, when Huggins removed some of the boxes, he'd taken them off the top of each row. It not only saved him from bending, but it also left the equivalent of large box-size steps. Tango's leap landed her on a box, two high, and after that, getting to the top of the stack was easy.

Very carefully, she peered over the edge, closest to the barn wall, and discovered, although it was a long way down, there was a small gap. Not only that, but she could smell the night air coming through their concealed hole, now four boxes below. Although Tango couldn't count, it was the actually an eight foot drop. All she knew that it was a very long way.

"What can you see?" Duke asked.

"I think I can do it," Tango replied.

"Tango," Vicky called quietly. "Tango, come here girl."

When she didn't reappear, Vicky tried to turn the chair, by pushing with her feet while attempting to jump. With great effort, she did manage to get the chair far enough sideways to see the wall of boxes, but there was still no sign of Tango.

She tried not to panic, or cry again.

Meanwhile, on top of the boxes, Tango was trying to decide what to do. If she went headfirst into the gap, she risked not only getting stuck, but also breaking her neck. So reminding herself that Vicky was in great danger, she turned and faced the wall with the door. Then she crouched, letting her back legs dangle over the drop, while she clawed frantically with her front paws as gravity took her over. Luckily, Corgis have longer than average claws, to give them a better grip when herding cows and sheep, and allowing them to turn with amazing speed. As Tango dropped into the dark, she was making full use of them. Huggins hadn't stacked the boxes perfectly, so there were small ledges that she caught with her claws, slowing her fall. Suddenly, she was at the bottom, their hidden hole only a foot away, but Tango was now stuck, effectively wedged between the barn wall and a box at the bottom of the stack.

She could hear Vicky calling her.

"Are you okay?" Duke barked.

"I'm at the bottom," came the muffled reply. "But I'm stuck."

"Wiggle! Wiggle a lot," Misty barked loudly. "Use your claws and dig!"

"You can do it!" Duke barked even louder. "You can! You can!"

With all those words of encouragement from her aunt and uncle, Tango began to frantically wiggle and push. With one supreme effort, she squeezed out of the narrow space, and found herself with clear access to the hole. To her relief, it had never been found, and as she stuck her head through, she could see the moonlight on the far side of the rusty drum.

"I'm free!" she called out.

"Get help," Duke barked back. "Find Jake and Skipper. Hurry!" Vicky clearly heard Tango bark, then there was silence.

Outside, in the cool night air, Tango realized that the only way she knew how to find Jake was to go to his office. And the only way she knew how to do that was to go home, and begin from there.

She was under the rusty barbed wire fence in record time, and used all her speed to cross the marsh in a straight line, heading toward their escape hole. Half way across, she almost collided with a red fox on his nightly hunt, making him duck down in surprise. As Tango leaped over him, she hardly slowed. When the fox did raise his head, the dog was long gone.

By the time she reached their escape hole, she was very wet and covered in thick black mud. Finally slowing, she suddenly realized that there was also no way out, if she entered the garden. So taking the time to control her heavy panting, she trotted along the outside of the fence. As soon as she reached the cottage driveway, she took off again along Marshside Road. The road was narrow, but after the bumpy, rough marsh grass, the blacktop was smooth as she raced along it, skidding to a halt at Jake's office door, a few minutes later.

But the sheriff's department was in darkness, and there was no sign of Jake and Skipper. Still panting hard, and very, very tired, she sat down, not knowing what to do next. In less than a minute, she was asleep.

Back at the farm, Phil had followed a narrow footpath, raised a foot above the marsh, dragging Dog behind him.

"Come on, you big brute," he said, jerking hard on Dog's leash. "Time to earn your keep."

To stop the pain in his neck, Dog decided the only way to stop it was to trot close to Phil's heels.

"That's a good dog," Phil continued. "I knew you'd see it my way."

Don't bet on it, Dog thought, trying to avoid the worst of the mud, and knowing that if he pulled Phil off the path, they could both get stuck in the boggy wet ground.

Dog heard the sound of an engine, long before they rounded a bend. As they got closer, he could see a faint light from a boat, tied to the remains of an old dock.

"That you, Phil?" a voice from the darkness asked quietly.

"It's me, Chuck."

"Everything okay?"

"So far," Phil added, climbing onboard, and giving Dog a huge tug, the Rottweiler was forced to follow.

Chuck immediately backed up when Dog landed in the boat. "Keep that monster under control," he said, beginning to untie the dock lines.

Dog grinned, showing his teeth, and could smell the man's fear.

As the boat floated away from the dock, Chuck stood at the helm, and put it in gear. It was then Dog realized that he had no plan to stop them.

When the boat's speed began to increase with the rumble of a powerful engine, Dog knew he'd have to act, otherwise they'd soon be leaving the tidal channels and reaching the sea.

With an angry bark, Dog lunged at Chuck, easily pulling Phil off his feet and forcing him to let go of the leash.

Chuck turned, just as the Rottweiler pounced, and to avoid the worse of Dog's attack, he let go of the wheel. Chuck tried to protect himself by shielding his face and body with his arms, giving Dog an easy target.

Any thought of cruising quietly away from the farm was immediately forgotten. With no one at the helm, and as Chuck went to his knees to avoid the worst of Dog's bites, the boat continued to gather speed.

Unseen by Dog, Chuck managed to grab a boat hook on a long pole and aim it in Dog's direction. Using only one hand to swing the boat hook, it had a lot less force behind it, but it still managed to pierce Dog's shoulder, making him yelp in pain. Dog backed up, blood now pouring from his wound, while Phil struggled to his feet. He was about to make a grab for Dog's collar, when he looked up.

In the darkness, the muddy side wall of the channel loomed  ahead of them, and forgetting Dog, he tried desperately to reach the wheel. But he was too late. The boat hit the bank, head on, and the impact was so great, it sent Phil flying through the air. With a loud splash, he hit the water.

Having both been thrown to the bottom of the boat, Chuck and Dog still heard Phil shout, "I can't swim!" above the sound of the still running engine.

Dog was not only hurt and bleeding, but also dazed from the impact. It was Chuck who recovered first, struggling to his feet, just as the boat broke free. With the engine still running, it careened across the channel, this time slamming sideways into the opposite muddy channel wall. The force of this impact sent the boat on its side, almost flipping it, and catapulting both Chuck and Dog into the dark murky water.

As Dog surfaced, instinct took over, and he immediately began to swim. A few feet ahead of him, Chuck was also swimming, and watching the now empty boat disappear into the darkness, with no one at the helm.

Dog kept his head high as the boat's wake hit him, while Chuck swam for the muddy bank. It was a mistake. As his feet touch bottom, he sank, being sucked down by the thick, sticky mud. He tried to struggle free, but it only made things worse. When Dog last saw him, before swimming across to the far side, Chuck was up to his chest in water, held captive by the mud.

Dog was in the water for several minutes, before he found a firm enough spot to drag himself out and up the muddy bank. The water had washed off a lot of the blood from the wound on his shoulder, but he was alive, and could still walk. He'd also been very smart. He'd reached dry land on the farm's side of the channel, and all he had to do now was get back there.

Sore and still bleeding, he limped through the marsh, his nose guiding his way. He was forced to stop, more than once, but eventually, the barn's large silhouette came thankfully into view.

In a deep sleep, outside Jake's office, Tango was sure she could smell fish.

"Are you okay?" a strange voice asked, the fishy smell now a lot stronger.

Deciding it wasn't a dream, after all, Tango opened her eyes to see a round, very furry face, with long whiskers and amazing green eyes, close to hers. Tango sat, and tried to get the strange looking creature into focus.

"I'm Tom," the creature added. "I live at the supermarket."

"I'm Tango," she replied. "Why's your nose so flat?"

"My father was a Persian," the creature replied in a way that made Tango realize that it was supposed to mean something special.

Until this moment, Tango had never seen a cat, and since moving to the cottage, no cat with any commonsense would come near the garden. And most cats had a lot of commonsense. She also knew that her siblings would chase them, if there had been any to chase.

Tom now stretched, showing off very long, sharp claws. "Are you looking for the sheriff?"

"Yes, and my big brother Skipper."

"Now I know who you are," Tom continued. "There was an accident, so the sheriff left."

Tango got to her feet, and noticed that she couldn't have been asleep very long as she was still wet and muddy. "How do you know that?"

"Some of the volunteer firefighters were at the supermarket when they heard about it. They all drove away in a hurry. Then I saw the sheriff's truck speeding down the road."

"Was Skipper with him?"

Tom began cleaning his whiskers. "I don't know. The truck was going too fast."

Tango shook, trying to ignore how tired she still was. "Which way?"

Tom arched his back, stretching again. "That way."

In an instant, Tango took off down the sidewalk along Main Street, quickly disappearing from view.

"You're welcome," Tom added, beginning to wash his paws. "Dogs really are crazy. And rude, too."

When the sidewalk ended, Tango used the road. She raced passed the supermarket's empty parking lot, and kept on going.

At 5:30 p.m., Jake had been about to lock up, when he got a call from the emergency dispatcher.

"There's been an auto accident outside Oaks Farm on rural route 102," the dispatcher said. "Fire and ambulance are already responding."

"Come on," Jake said immediately to Skipper. "We've got to go."

He called Vicky on his way to the scene, lights and siren on, but there was no reply from her cell phone. When he called the cottage, he got the answering machine, and left a message to tell her why Skipper was going to be late home.

"I expect she's in the garden," he said, as the SUV came to a halt.

Jake left Skipper in the SUV, as he approached the mangled wreck. Mrs. Foster, it appeared, well known for being absentminded, had been too busy talking on her cell phone, as she rounded the blind bend, to see the tractor and trailer backing out of the farm gate.

Her small car hit the trailer, wedging in underneath, with Mrs. Foster still behind the wheel. Although she was saved from any serious injury by the air bags, she was also trapped.

"We're going to have to cut her out," one of the firefighters said to Jake as he approached. "And it's going to take sometime."

With no way passed the accident that effectively blocked the road, Jake spent the next several hours, diverting traffic, while the firefighters went to work on freeing Mrs. Foster from the tangled metal.

When Mrs. Foster was finally removed from what remained of her car, and driven away in a ambulance, sirens blaring, Tango was just a few hundred yards away. When she heard the noise, she ran faster.

When she skidded to a halt at the side of Jake's SUV, the road flares were being put out, and the fire trucks were getting ready to leave.

"Skipper!" Tango barked. "Mom's been kidnapped!"

His head immediately appeared through the open window, looking down. "Where?"

"At the farm," Tango replied. "We've got to help her. Jump!"

Regardless of the risk, Skipper did just that, landing on all four paws. The fact that Jake had parked on the grass at the side of the road, helped greatly with the impact.

Over the noise of engines and men shouting, Jake clearly heard a bark he recognized. He turned toward his SUV, just in time to see Skipper jump out, and Tango by his side. Before he could react, the dogs sped away, and around the bend, disappearing from view.

Jake didn't hesitate. He ran to the SUV, and putting it quickly in gear, his hit the gas peddle. Grass and dirt flew up from the spinning tires, but as soon they touched the blacktop with a loud squeal, he was off in hot pursuit.

As fast as the dogs were running, it didn't take Jake long to see them in the headlights, many yards ahead of him.

He backed off on the gas, just as the headlights from another vehicle came into view.

His heart missed at beat when he realized that the driver would see the dogs too late, but Skipper and Tango, sensing danger, moved to the side of the road as the vehicle sped passed them.

It was also passed Jake in a flash, but he was sure he saw Huggins behind the wheel of the speeding red pickup.

Time for him later, he thought, still keeping Skipper and Tango in view.

At Huggins' farm, they turned down the rutted track, and Jake knew that he'd been smart to follow them.

"I'm back!" Dog barked, staggering to the rear of the barn.

"We're still here," Duke barked back. "Did you see Tango?"

"No," he replied. "She's not with you?"

"She went to get help," Misty called out.

Vicky knew that from the Corgis reaction, something or someone was on the other side of the barn wall.

"I'm in here," she shouted. "Help me. Help me, please!"

"What can I do?" Dog asked.

"Find a way to get to us," Duke replied. "The hole Tango made is too small, and the door is locked."

Dog studied the barn's old planking in the moonlight. "The hole you first made is still here. I can try and make it bigger?"

"Do it!," Duke barked.

To Vicky's amazement and then increasing uneasiness, whatever was on the far side of the barn was now trying to break in. She could hear grunting and panting, as slowly, the lower planks began to move. The sounding of wood breaking was unmistakable as the hole grew larger, big enough for Vicky to see Huggins' huge dog on the other side.

Dog gave one more huge effort, his jaws clamping down hard, as he gripped another plank. With a tearing sound, it finally gave way, making a hole large enough for him to finally squeeze through.

I'm going to die, Vicky thought, as the huge wet dog, covered in blood, and droll dripping from his enormous jaws came toward her.

But before she could scream, Duke stepped forward, blocking his way.

"Thank you," Duke said, touching Dog's nose with his own. "You're hurt?"

Dog shook, sending drool in an arc, but this time, Misty didn't duck. She also touched Dog's nose. "Our Mom needs your help," she said. "Are you going to be okay?"

"Just a few scratches," Dog replied, shaking again. "Show me how."

It was now obvious to Vicky that the dogs not only knew each other, but were friends, although she couldn't imagine how.

Her fear immediately subsided, as Dog limped to the back of her chair, and began carefully gnawing on the knots that bound her hands.

"Good boy. Good boy. Keep going."

Vicky thought that Duke and Misty were just barking encouragement, as Dog began to get the knots loose, but they'd both heard Skipper and Tango, quickly followed by the sound of Jake's SUV.

Jumping from the SUV, Jake followed the dogs into the barn, to find them barking and scratching furiously at the stack of rotting hay bales. He could also hear Duke and Misty on the other side, and from then on, it didn't take him long to find the camouflaged door. Breaking off the padlock with the butt of his gun, Jake flung the door open to find Vicky untying some rope around her ankles, being watched by Dog. On seeing Jake, Skipper and Tango, Duke and Misty went wild.

"Are you okay?" he asked above the noise of the sibling's enthusiastic greeting.

"Yes," she said as he reached her, and helped her to stand. "The dogs saved me. Can you…"

She didn't finish the sentence as Jake kissed her and then held her tight. And this time, Skipper didn't object.

Suddenly, the couple realized that the room had gone very quiet.

Vicky turned to see Dog, lying on his side, covered in blood and sweat, and not moving.

Jake was by his side in an instant.

"He's still alive," he said. "But he's lost a lot of blood. We've got to get him to Doc. Metzer, right now. You can tell me what happened on the way."

Very carefully, Jake and Vicky carried Dog to the SUV, placing him gently on the rear seat. As Tango was too tired to jump in after Skipper, Duke and Misty, Vicky picked her up.

Tango was already asleep, as Jake drove as fast as he dare away from the farm, already calling the local veterinarian, Dr. Metzer, and getting him out of bed. His second call was to Hank, telling him to secure the farm and bring reinforcements.

"Where's Huggins?" Hank asked.

"I'm not sure," Jake replied, and then remembered the speeding pickup. "Right now, he's not my priority."

It was good for all concerned that Dr. Metzers' office was at his house. He met them in the driveway, dressed in pajamas and a robe, flashlight in hand.

On seeing Jake, all the Corgis, with Tango asleep, cradled in Vicky's arms, he didn't object when everyone crowed into his small examination room.

He took his time to check out Dog.

"That's a nasty deep flesh wound, " he said finally, "But with a few stitches and a lot of rest, I don't see why he won't be as good as new. He's a brave dog."

"They all are," Jake replied. "If it hadn't been for the Corgis, Vicky might still be tied up, or worse."

Jake helped Dr. Metzer with Dog, while Vicky took a seat, Tango still asleep in her arms, Skipper, Duke and Misty laying quietly at her feet.

Eventually, Dog was placed in a large crate with blankets and a water bowl.

"He'll sleep for several hours because of the anesthetic," Dr. Metzer said, closing the door. "But he looks like he could use it." He turned to Vicky. "Seeing as I'm now wide awake, do you need me to check out your dogs?"

"Yes, please," she replied. "Skipper first. But I need to hold him, unless you want to lose an arm?"

"How comforting," Dr. Metzer muttered, as Vicky handed a very limp Tango to Jake.

Thankfully, in Vicky's mind, Skipper behaved himself, and neither he, Duke or Misty seemed any the worse for their ordeal. Tango however, according to Dr. Metzer was suffering from exhaustion.

"She's really cute," he added. "My best advise is to let her sleep, and then clean her up later. In the meantime, the Rottweiler will be quite safe here."

"I'm taking you home," Jake said back at the SUV. "I've got to find Huggins and his accomplices. Okay with you?"

"It's fine," she replied. "We all need the sleep, and with the dogs to protect me, I've got no need to worry."

Just like Mrs. Foster, Huggins wasn't paying enough attention as he sped away from the farm, more concerned with his escape than he was with his driving. He knew he'd passed the sheriff, going in the opposite direction, and was surprised when he didn't turn around to follow.

Just as I thought, small town sheriff, Huggins was thinking as he flipped open his cell phone to dial. Distracted, and going far too fast, he misjudged the blind bend. The pickup went into a skid, as Huggins wrestled with the wheel. And he might have succeeded in controlling it, had it not been for the fact that, in the dark, the firefighters had missed cleaning up a small patch of oil. The pickup hit the oil, and flipped several times, before landing upside down in the ditch, it's tires still spinning.

When two hours later, Jake saw the wreck in the headlights of the SUV, he immediately stopped.

Not again, he thought. "Stay in the truck," he ordered Vicky, now recognizing the pickup.

But Skipper sensed an opportunity, and leapt through Jake's open door, before anyone could stop him. Then he raced across the road and into the ditch.

Huggins was knocked unconscious in the wreck. But when he woke up, he found he was hanging upside down in his tightly locked seatbelt, the driver's door too badly damaged to open. He wasn't sure how long he'd been there, squashed against the roof of the pickup's cab, when he thought he heard something. Managing to painfully turn his head, he came face to face, through the broken window, with a very angry dog. Skipper was snarling, showing off sharp white teeth, and his hackles and ruff raised to their full extent as he edged even closer, smelling the man's fear.

Huggins was already yelling for help, as Jake slithered into the ditch.

"Want me to call off the dog?" Jake asked.

"Yes! Yes!" Huggins shouted.

"Before I do, where are the others?"

"On a boat heading for Charleston." Huggins could feel Skipper's hot breath. "Do something! He's going to kill me."

"I wouldn't blame him," Jake replied, and then called Skipper away.

Skipper sat, watching Jake cut Huggins out of the seatbelt, before dragging him through the broken window. Then he handcuffed him, and pulled him out of the ditch. Huggins was scratched and bruised, but otherwise unharmed, as he was pushed in the direction of the SUV, with Skipper now close on his heels.

"Sorry," Jake said to Vicky at the door of the truck. "I've got to take him to jail. No passengers."

"That's fine with me," she replied, climbing out, still cradling Tango. She glared at Huggins. "I much rather walk."

Huggins was about to respond, when the growls of three Corgis stopped him.

"Wait here," Jake said to her, before driving away. "I'll be back soon."

As the dawn broke, Vicky was finally asleep in her bed, surrounded by the Corgis. Throughout it all, Tango hadn't woken up, and although she was still covered in mud, it was now dry, along with her fur.

"That was quite a day," Duke whispered, before his eyes closed.

"If that wasn't the classic understatement, I don't know what is," Misty murmured.

Skipper remained silent, and wasn't about to sleep, until he was sure that everyone in the bedroom was now quite safe.

CHAPTER SIXTEEN

NOT SURPRISINGLY, EVERYONE SLEPT in.

By the time Jake arrived at the cottage, Vicky hadn't been up long, but was in the process of finally washing the mud off Tango in the utility room sink.

She lifted her out, wrapped in a big fluffy towel, and then kissed Jake.

Skipper watched. He was now used to Jake entering the cottage without ringing the bell, and he noted that Vicky seemed really happy to see him.

"Give her to me," Jake said, taking the wet furry bundle. "Dr. Metzer's right. You are cute."

Dog thinks so too, Tango thought, as Jake rubbed her dry.

"What's happening?" Vicky asked.

"Someone from the FBI is coming to get Huggins, later today."

"Good riddance," Vicky replied.

"I couldn't agree more. Dr. Metzer called, this morning," Jake continued. "He's says the Rottweiler's making a good recovery, and can leave tomorrow."

"Leave for where?" Vicky asked. "He's got nowhere to go."

Jake didn't reply.

"You want him to come here?" she continued to Jake's silence. "You do, don't you?"

"Only until we can find him a good home. He seems to get on well with the Corgis"

"Fine," she said. "But its only temporary, you understand."

"No problem," he replied, heading to the door. "See you tonight?"

"I'm counting on it."

As Jake opened the door, Skipper bolted, making straight for the SUV.

"He's in a routine," Vicky said.

"The investigation isn't over. So if it's okay with you?"

She laughed. "See you both tonight."

What Jake hadn't told Vicky was that in his earlier call from Dr. Metzer, the veterinarian had also asked where the Rottweiler had come from.

Jake told him.

"Did you know the dog was micro-chipped?" Metzer continued.

"No way I would."

"Well I don't know how Huggins got him. According to his chip, his name is Benny, and his owner lives in West Palm Beach."

"Florida?"

"That's right." Metzer then gave Jake the name of Benny's owner, along with his address and phone number.

But when Jake called the number, he got a recording that said the number was no longer in service. Wanting to check on Vicky and the Corgis, Jake fully intended doing a lot more research when he got back to his office.

With Skipper laying by Jake's chair, his deputy badge in full view on his collar, Jake began his research with the computer. Accessing information that was only available to law enforcement, Jake did discover, to his relief, that David Ross, Benny's owner, didn't have a criminal record. But he didn't find out any more information, including the fact that David Ross didn't have a Florida driver's license either.

"Try the military," Hank said, when Jake mention that fact. "They're always on the move."

Why didn't I think of that? Jake thought, beginning the search again. *I'm losing my touch*

But thirty minutes later, Jake found that David Ross was a sergeant in the Army, stationed at Fort Benning, Georgia. He called the base commander. Jake was transferred several times, but after an hour, when he finally hung up, he had a lot more information. David Ross was now serving in Iraq, and not able to find a family member to take the large Rottweiler, he'd been forced to hand Benny over for adoption.

And Huggins said he was from West Palm Beach. It all makes sense, Jake thought.

At 3:00 p.m., the office door opened, and a man in a dark suit entered. Skipper didn't react, but was on alert, as the man approached Jake' s desk, grinning broadly.

"You look good in a sheriff's uniform," the man said, before giving Jake a big hug.

Hank and Skipper watched closely.

"Meet Special Agent Frank Robbins, FBI," Jake said to Hank. "He's my brother."

"Good to meet you," Hank replied. "That explains a lot."

Frank then bent down, facing Skipper. "Is this the hero?"

"More like super star," Jake replied.

Knowing that Frank was Jake's brother, Skipper stepped forward, and sat.

"Nice to meet you, too, Skipper," Frank said. "From what I've been told, it sounds like you deserve a medal." He stroked Skipper's head. "What a good looking dog."

"Don't mention his size," Jake said quickly.

Frank stood. "I wasn't going to. I wish I could stay, but we've got prisoners to move."

"I know," Jake replied. "It's this way."

After Hank had been instructed to get reinforcements, he'd done just that.

A large group of police officers had arrived at the farm to begin a search. Several hours later, using tracker dogs, they found Chuck, up to his waist in mud in the tidal channel. It was lucky for Chuck, everyone thought, that the tide was now low, otherwise he could well have drowned. Not able to get a vehicle through the marsh to pull him out, several officers got extremely wet and dirty, as roped to other officers and using planks of wood from the farm, they were forced to dig him out.

Even though Phil couldn't swim, he'd managed, in his panic, to dog paddle to an area of bushes on the bank. At high tide and in the dark, he hadn't seen the bush's long roots stretching deep into the water. As he began to haul himself out, his foot got tangled in the roots, and with muddy wet hands, he lost his grip. When the searchers found him, he was still stuck in the jumble of roots, with a broken ankle. He was carried on a stretcher to a waiting ambulance, while Chuck Gaston joined Ralph Huggins in the prison cells at the sheriff's department.

The searchers also discovered the boat, it's engine still running, stuck in the mud, a quarter of a mile away. Under a tarp in the rear of the boat, they also found many cardboard boxes with the words, 'Paper Towel' imprinted on the outside. But the boxes were full of small clear plastic bags, filled with a white powder, that on closer examination looked remarkably like heroin. If that was the case, they calculated the street value at almost a million dollars.

Jake now opened a heavy steel door, with a small window, and with Frank close behind, they entered the cells.

Two men, both wearing bright orange overalls, turned.

"Hello, Gerry," Frank said to Huggins. "I told you, it would only be a matter of time." He then faced an astonished Jake. "Meet Gerald Thomas of New York City. How long have we known each other, Gerry?"

The man known as Ralph Huggins refused to answer and only glared.

"But this is really Chuck Gaston," Frank continued. "A known Thomas accomplice. And with these guys now under lock and key, the streets and our kids will be a lot safer."

With Jake's help, both men were shackled, and lead through the office and out to where two dark Suburbans and several more FBI agents were waiting at the curb.

Skipper's last act, as the man he knew as Huggins passed him, was to snarl and show his teeth, but this time, there was no comment from the man in shackles, although he did shuffle faster to avoid the angry Corgi.

"Good work, bro," Frank said on the sidewalk. "I owe you."

"And don't be a stranger," Jake replied. "Just call me next time you want to bring a major drug dealer to justice."

"I'll remember that." Frank was grinning broadly as the door to the Suburban closed.

Skipper watched from the doorway, as the vehicles went down Main Street and disappeared from view

"They're gone," Jake told Skipper. "But this investigation still isn't quite over."

"How come?" Hank asked, as Skipper lay down at the side of Jake's desk again.

"Ralph Huggins was a real person. I need to know how Thomas was able to take his identity. And I start in West Palm Beach."

Chapter Seventeen

In the weeks that followed, and with Vicky's agreement, Skipper continued to accompany Jake to his office on Monday through Friday, but over the weekend, he stayed home with Vicky and his siblings.

The day after Gerald Thomas and Chuck Gaston were taken away by the FBI, Vicky went to get Benny from Dr. Metzer. Jake finally told her about his background, and for his part, Benny was making a good recovery, and delighted to be with his friends in a loving home again.

As far as the humans were concerned, Benny was a very sweet dog, and not at all vicious. He was also very attached to Tango, and they were virtually inseparable. When he'd recovered sufficiently, and his stitches had been removed, they could be seen chasing squirrels together, much to Misty's dismay.

"Don't worry," Duke told her. "Benny isn't going to be here forever. You'll get your playmate back, eventually."

"How do you know that?"

"Skipper told me. Jake's still trying to find out how Benny got adopted."

Misty wasn't convinced, as she walked away in search of small lizards to chase.

Jake spent many hours researching Ralph Huggins. Now knowing he was originally from West Palm Beach, he began to make progress.

With lawyer, Mike Burton's help, they discovered that the real Ralph Huggins had actually died suddenly of a heart attack. While looking for a false identity, they assumed that Thomas had read the obituaries, and found that Huggins was not only roughly the same age, but also seemed to have no living relatives, except for distant cousin Bubba Smith, of Cobbs Creek, Georgia.

To make doubly sure that Bubba wasn't going to be a problem, Thomas went to find him, and discovered that the old man's farm was a ideal location for his drug dealing. It came out later, at Thomas' trial, that at first, he'd asked the farmer to sell him the property. But Bubba had no intention of ever selling. A huge argument began, and when Thomas physically threatened Bubba, he tried to escape through the marsh, an area he knew very well. Being so much younger, Thomas had no trouble catching him. It was at that point, the Corgis saw what happened next.

With his underworld contacts, it was then easy for Thomas to get all the necessary fake documents to assume the real Huggins' identity. Although Skipper wasn't at the trial, Jake was, and he made sure, in his testimony, that Skipper and his siblings were given full credit for bringing Thomas and his criminal network to justice.

News of the dog's involvement spread like wildfire through TV, newspaper headlines and especially the Internet. The story quickly got worldwide attention, and for the third time, Cobbs Creek became the focus of film crews. Acting on Vicky's behalf, lawyer, Mike Burton, threatened to sue WQRXTV, and Jenny Beale in particular, for putting Vicky's life at risk with Jenny's reporting of the original story. So when the news broke again, it was John Mayhew whom viewers saw behind the news desk. Having refused the demotion to network weather girl, Jenny, soon left for parts unknown.

In the hope that all the attention would soon go away, Vicky reluctantly did give one short interview, and allowed the dogs to be filmed. But Mayor Cobb, Polly Parker, Dolores Black and Ernie, the mail carrier, were only too happy to be in front of the cameras again. It was really good for business.

Jake had continued to dig into the real Huggins' background and eventually found the West Palm Beach lawyer who was handling his estate.

"I found out he has a daughter," the lawyer told Jake. "But I've been unsuccessful in tracking her down. I'm not sure she's even aware that her father is dead."

That news surprised Jake. If what the lawyer said was true, whoever she was had just inherited the farm.

After the remaining drugs had been removed from the secret room, behind the rotting hay bales, to keep reporters away, Jake and Hank repaired the old gate, and kept it chained shut. When the news crews first arrived in Cobbs Creek, an officer from a neighboring police department, stood on duty at the gate, to keep everyone out.

But as Jake was about to discover, the Internet has its uses. Two weeks after the trial ended, and it became yesterdays news, the door to Jake's office opened, and a young woman entered.

Skipper immediately sat, watching closely as she approached Jake's desk.

"Sheriff Robbins?" she asked, and held out her hand. "I'm Ralph Huggins daughter, Patricia."

Jake was flabbergasted. "Nice to meet you," he replied. "I'm very sorry about your father."

"Thank you. And cousin Bubba, I understand. What a terrible thing to happen. My father's estate lawyer told me to come and see you."

Jake was about to learn that Patricia Huggins graduated university with a degree in zoology. With a desire to protect endangered spies from extinction, she'd been hired by a privately funded foundation, and soon found herself as a member of a team that was sent to Indonesia. Her father had objected strongly to her going overseas to such an out of the way place that could possibly be dangerous, and they had not parted on the best of terms. The only way the estate lawyer found out about Patricia, was an occasional letter she'd sent her father that the lawyer found amongst his possessions. Patricia's father was correct in assuming that the islands had very little outside communication. Away from the bigger cities, and deep in the jungle, even the Internet didn't work. Patricia had been there for the past eighteen months, and it was only because a fellow team member, on a trip back to civilization to get supplies, accessed the Internet and read the story, that she knew what had happened. It had then taken Patricia almost two weeks to get back to the United States.

"So here I am," she finished.

"Where are you staying?" Jake asked.

"The local Bed and Breakfast. Mrs. Foster seems really sweet."

"And absentminded," Hank muttered.

With Skipper having to sit on the back seat, behind the wire mesh containment barrier of the sheriff's department SUV, Jake drove Patricia to the farm. Jake and Skipper had checked up on the property at least once a week since Thomas' arrest, but with no one living there, the farm had gone from bad to worse. The new stainless steel appliances were still in the kitchen, but apart from that, and rooms of Bubba's old furniture, the farmhouse was a dilapidated mess.

Patty, as she told Jake to call her, really surprised him. "It's fabulous," she commented, looking around in the courtyard.

"You haven't seen the inside," he replied.

Patty studied the house. "I'm going to need a lot of help remodeling it, that's for sure."

That comment gave Jake an idea as he immediately thought of Vicky and the cottage. "And I know a person who can really help you."

"How many acres did you say?" Patty asked.

"Forty-six," Jake continued. "But some of that's marsh and tidal channels."

"Perfect for wildlife."

And us, Skipper thought.

Two nights later, at Vicky's invitation, Patty was enjoying dinner at the cottage, and the company of five dogs. It became quickly apparent that she'd fallen for the big, friendly Rottweiler, while Benny felt an immediate connection with the pretty young woman.

"I've given the matter a lot of thought," Patty said, after the meal was over. "When I went off to university, my father sold the family home, and moved to a one bedroom apartment. Admittedly, it has a spectacular view of the ocean, but it's not for me. I much prefer the country and some space."

"You'll certainly get that at the farm," Vicky replied.

"I'd like to make it a working farm again," Patty continued. "I think my great, great grandparent's would approve, do you?"

"I'm sure they would."

Patty looked around. "The cottage is so beautiful. Jake told me you did all this?"

Vicky nodded. "I like remodeling, I guess."

"You're an expert. The farmhouse needs a complete make-over. So if I asked really nicely, would you help me? Please?"

"It also needs a dog," Vicky said.

"I agree," Patty continued. "I'll adopt Benny, if you'll help me out?"

"That sounds like blackmail," Jake commented.

"But the best possible kind."

"I'll do it," Vicky added. "On the condition that the dogs all get together on a regular basis."

"You've got a deal," Patty replied.

"Oh, goody," Tango whispered from underneath the table.

Chapter Eighteen

Before Patty returned to West Palm Beach, to sell her late father's apartment, but leaving Benny temporarily with Vicky, she hired Vicky's contractors to start work on the farmhouse.

"This way, I'll have a new roof over my head, when I come back," she said. "If you can live in all that mess, I can too. I'm also used to camping out."

As it turned out, it was just as well.

A few days later, Mrs. Foster forgot about a pan of stew on the stove, and went shopping. The firefighters managed to save most of the Bed and Breakfast from the fire, but until the house was repaired and cleaned from all the smoke damage, Mrs. Foster wouldn't be taking anymore paying guests.

Patty wasn't away long, and in the months that followed, with Benny at her side, she moved permanently to the farm. Vicky kept her word, so she and the Corgis were frequent visitors, as the remodeling progressed.

Skipper, who still hated loud noises, kept out of the house, and spent most of the time checking out the old milking shed and barn with his siblings and Benny. Just as he suspected, Misty and Tango were gleeful at the prospect of chasing all the furry inhabitants and making their lives miserable.

To everyone's surprise, John Mayhew, now a TV news anchor and another local celebrity, sold the newspaper to Dolores Black.

"May as well turn a hobby into a paying business," she said. "Small town newspapers rely on gossip. And who better than me."

No one in town disagreed.

As Dolores had no intention of getting rid of the garden center and flower shop, she hired an editor to manage the newspaper.

With the small town being featured on the news on more than one occasion during the proceeding year, Cobbs Creek attracted many more tourists. So much so, that when the Fire Marshall refused to renew Mrs. Foster's Bed and Breakfast permit, citing her absentminded behavior as the main reason, Mayor Cobb seized the chance, and turned his ancestral home into a small hotel.

Many tourists now traveled to the pretty coastal town, so it was the law of averages that some of them wanted to make Cobbs Creek their permanent home. Some of the older houses got sold to the newcomers, and in a few cases, some of them were lucky enough to find land on which to build.

As the town expanded, Jake had to hire another deputy, although he still maintained that Cobbs Creek had the lowest crime rate of anywhere in the country.

Skipper's time with Jake at his office was slowly decreased, as he spent more and more time with Vicky while she finished her fourth book, and immediately began book five. Jake didn't need to ask what it was about. Happy to be back with Mom, although Skipper missed the sheriff's department, he eventually he got used to just staying home. He was, however, allowed to keep his deputy badge.

"In case he ever needs it again," Jake said.

"That's highly unlikely," Vicky replied.

Almost twelve months after Skipper, Duke, Misty and Tango saw Bubba Smith's murder, Jake and Vicky, with Skipper by her side, now watched the setting sun at the cottage fence. As the sun disappeared below the horizon, leaving behind a sky of orange and gold, Vicky looked across the marsh to the farm.

"What do I do about the dog's escape route?" she quietly asked him.

Jake put his arm around her shoulders. "They don't know you found it?"

MISTY

We do now, Skipper thought. Vicky shook her head.

"Then leave it," he replied. "It gives them access to Benny. If they're missing, at least we'll know where they are."

A few feet away, Misty, who was searching for lizards to chase, immediately went to find her brother and niece to tell them the news.

"So, they found it," Duke said. "They're not stupid. I kept telling you that."

"But what happens if Mom does decide to block the hole?" Misty asked.

Tango grinned. "I'll dig a bigger one. I'm now older and a lot stronger."

Duke had heard enough, and trotted off in Jake and Vicky's direction.

"So what's the plan now?" he asked, reaching Skipper.

"I'm working on it."

"Of course, you are," Duke replied. "Why did I expect anything less."

About The Author

CAROLYN EASTWOOD WAS BORN and educated in England, and grew up with her first Corgi. When she moved to the United States, and later became a U.S. citizen, she brought her second Corgi with her. Half way through a corporate career, she got the "writing bug," and quit her job to write a People of Interest column for a well-known Connecticut newspaper. After winning the annual Maryland Writers' Association Fiction Contest in 1999, she began a fact-based crime/military thriller series for adults. The first book was published in 2003, the second in 2006, and the third in 2013. In between, there were more Corgis. She says that watching the interaction between the siblings featured in this book was the perfect platform for a series of Corgi mysteries aimed at Tweens and all Corgi loving adults.

Find out more about the author and the Corgis at:

www.mycorgidogs.com